The Day
I Stopped Worrying
and
Learned to Love
Berkeley Hunt

A light comedy and a farcical satire on
geopolitics, corruption, and finance

Peter Rauth

ISBN: 978-0-244-02255-6

Cover artwork by Rick Coleman: www.caricature.co.uk

Contact the author at:
Peter.Rauth@Hotmail.com.

PublishNation
www.publishnation.co.uk

First for dearest Pamela.
For little Carlotta.
And my good friends
Klaudiusz Pyczel,
and Max.

Prologue

In an alternate reality, remarkably similar to our own world, mankind is beset by many of the challenges we ourselves face on our own planet: the challenges of climate change and the environment, famine, economic and financial chaos, war, and civil unrest. Humanity looks on despairingly in the hope that those who lead them will bring them out of the darkness into the light.

Day One

A man is lying on a bed, to which he is handcuffed. He is attired in bondage leathers and has a small orange in his mouth. A woman, whose name is Penny, is at the end of the bed with a whip. She is similarly attired, but is devoid of any type of fruit.

Snarling, she barks, "You miserable worm … You deserve every lash that is coming to you." Just as she is about to flagellate the man a mobile phone rings. Exasperated, the man spits out the orange and gestures the woman to grab the offending device.

The man answers his phone and hears a female voice.

"I have Sir Percy Talleewacker for you, Prime Minister."

The Cabinet Secretary is connected.

"Prime Minister, you do remember that you have a meeting with the Scottish first minister in twenty minutes?"

"What? Err … yes … no. I … I mean I'd forgotten. I'll be right there," replies Berkeley Hunt. After putting down the phone he hurriedly unchains himself, but is unable to remove one handcuff from his wrist.

He curses, "Oh, God."

A few minutes later Berkeley Hunt emerges from this establishment of some considerable repute, it must be said, if you like that sort of thing. He is now attired in a business suit. The handcuff, however, is still attached to his hand and buried in his jacket pocket, where it remains unseen. A personal protection officer

(PPO) opens the door to his car and Berkeley Hunt gets in. The car moves off, accompanied by a police motorcycle escort.

Berkeley Hunt gazes out of the window as the car drives through Hyde Park. He passes a hand through his mop of unruly blonde hair and then pensively scratches the pale skin on his jowly cheek. His blue eyes barely register the beauty of a crisp, clear early spring day. Ruefully reflecting on the thought of a pleasure forgone, he sighs deeply. Overweight as a child, long before morbidly obese children became fashionable, Berkeley Hunt was mercilessly taunted by the other boys at his prep school. Even today, and in spite of his tailor's best efforts, he is unable to hide his somewhat rotund frame.

Berkeley Hunt is in his late forties. He doesn't really want to be prime minister and is not entirely certain as to how fate conspired to bring about such an unfortunate state of affairs. In fact, he doesn't really want to be anything, nor does he want to do anything except to be left alone. In spite of these obvious defects he endeavours to discharge his duties to the best of his woefully lacking abilities and, if possible, to do the right thing.

The prime minister's car stops at the gates to Downing Street. Before they can be stopped by the police a group of small children rush forward and begin hurling rotten fruit and vegetables at the car. The gates are opened and the prime minister's car speeds towards Number 10. Berkeley Hunt emerges, hand still buried in his jacket pocket. He ignores the questions from the gathered journalists and hurriedly enters Number 10.

Sir Percy Talleewacker, the Cabinet Secretary, greets Berkeley Hunt inside Number 10.

"What the bloody hell was all that about?" exclaims Berkeley Hunt.

"What do you mean?" asks Sir Percy.

"The children hurling fruit and veg at my car."

"Ah, I suspect it has something to do with the leaked proposals for next year's budget from the Chancellor's office about taxing children on their income. You know: pocket money, paper rounds … that sort of thing."

"What? I didn't know anything about that," exclaims Berkeley Hunt.

"I believe the Chancellor was going to announce it to the Cabinet tomorrow."

"What sort of hare-brained idea is that, anyway? And why do *I* get the blame for it?" he says, clearly exasperated.

"I agree, but as prime minister ultimately it is you who have to bear the brunt of people's outrage."

Berkeley Hunt throws his hands in the air and exhales deeply.

"Right. Well, anyway, I'd better go and see Mrs Turbot."

A few minutes later Berkeley Hunt is sitting in the Cabinet Room. His hand is still firmly in his jacket pocket. He is waiting for Patricia Turbot, the Scottish first minister. He is both expectant and nervous, as he is more than a little infatuated with her.

She enters the room with her aide, Malcolm. Forty-five years old, she is a handsome, desirable woman. For Berkeley Hunt time slows down, and he watches her in slow motion as she walks towards him. She is wearing an above-the-knee skirt and is showing rather more cleavage than would normally be appropriate. She tosses her head seductively, causing her long hair to caress her face. For a split second Berkeley Hunt imagines her dressed as a dominatrix with a whip, and he can barely control himself from having a spontaneous emission. He grabs hold of his genitals tightly.

Patricia Turbot and Malcolm take a seat.

"I'm terribly sorry I'm late. I was—"

Interrupting him, Patricia Turbot says, "That's quite all right, Prime Minister. I'm sure you were *very* tied up."

Berkeley Hunt turns slightly red, as he is not sure whether she is teasing him and is aware of his little secret. He continues, "Err …

4

Well, I suppose congratulations are in order at your by-election success—"

He is interrupted once more, this time by Malcolm.

"Success! From your side it makes the Charge of the Light Brigade look like the Battle of Agincourt. It was a massacre. You were totally decimated."

"What? Who the devil are you, and what do you mean by that?" replies the flustered prime minister.

"I'm terribly sorry, Prime Minister," says Patricia Turbot soothingly. She turns to Malcolm and fixes him with an admonishing glare. "This is Malcolm, my new aide and research assistant. I'm sure he didn't mean to be quite so ill-mannered. Did you, Malcolm?"

"That's all right, Patricia, but please call me Berkeley," he replies, attempting to regain his composure and inject as much charm as he can muster. "Well, what do you mean by that remark, young man?"

"The Scottish Independence Party," begins Malcolm, "won the seat and polled 37,000 votes in an *English* constituency. *Your* party got twenty-one votes. So your supporters wouldn't even have been able to put on a football match! What does that tell you?"

"Obviously it wasn't a good day for us, but I'm sure we'll rebound ... So what's your point?" says Berkeley Hunt, trying to sound assured.

"My point, Prime Minister, is that English capitalists would rather be governed by Scottish socialists, than the rabble you call your party and government. In fact the fringe party, Euthanasia for UK, polled twenty-two votes, which means that there are more Englishman in the constituency who would prefer to commit suicide than have you in government."

"That's enough, Malcolm," interjects Patricia Turbot. "I think it best if you leave the prime minister and me alone."

"But—"

He is interrupted once more by the Scottish first minister, "Now." She gives him a very hard stare. Malcolm gets up. His expression is a mixture of bewilderment and anger. He gives Berkeley Hunt a contemptuous look before he leaves.

"Funny ... wouldn't have tagged him as a Sweat— err ... Scot," says Berkeley Hunt.

"Well, public school and Oxbridge will do that for you, I suppose," replies Patricia Turbot.

"Ironic. Two institutions – ancient bastions of English culture and civilisation – and what happens? They throw out a Marxist revolutionary Scottish separatist. Oh, well," he replies.

"I am terribly sorry about his behaviour, Berkeley. He's young and passionate and genuinely believes that the 'wicked' English are oppressing his countrymen," says Patricia Turbot.

She crosses her legs slowly and deliberately so that her skirt rides up, revealing more of her thighs. Again, she deliberately folds her arms, accentuating the magnificence of her cleavage, and moves closer to Berkeley Hunt, such that her bosoms are only two feet away from his face. Tiny beads of perspiration appear on his brow. He resists the urge to wipe them off, but is beginning to lose the battle of resisting the urge to gaze at her glorious bust.

"Err ... Anyway, I'm sure *you* don't regard the English as wicked and oppressive," he replies.

"Of course not," she says gently, and turns her head away on purpose, as though deep in thought, giving Berkeley Hunt the opportunity to gawp at her cleavage for a few seconds unnoticed, or so he thinks.

She returns her gaze to the prime minister, who immediately reverts his eyes to meet hers as she continues to speak.

"However, in light of our election victory we do now have some serious issues to discuss. Now I appreciate that the election result was a bit of a freak and your party probably wouldn't have done quite so badly had it not been revealed that your candidate was such

– aah – an *ardent* animal lover. I believe the RSPCA are pressing charges. Nonetheless, the question of a new independence referendum has raised its head."

"Well, I'm not so sure, Patricia. I don't think there would be enough cross-party support for it. I'm not even convinced that you Swea — err … Scots really want one. And, of course, there's all this Brexit business still to deal with. But if you reconsidered your position on the tax reform bill I might be able to do something for you."

"I'm afraid I couldn't do that, Berkeley. You know there is even support in your *own* party for the bill. On the other hand, the SIP could just keep contesting by-elections in English constituencies and we may just put up candidates in *all* the English seats at the next general election. Who knows? On current performance the whole of the UK could eventually be governed from Scotland."

"Now I know you're only joking with me, Patricia, and even if I thought it was a good idea it may well take some time."

"Well … what would it take for *me* to convince you that it was a good idea?" she asks, injecting some sexiness into her voice. She places her hand on Berkeley Hunt's hand. He now begins to sweat profusely as she gently caresses it, and she continues,

"You know, I'm sure there's something that you would *really* like me to do to you … I mean *for* you, other than tax reform. Do you have any suggestions?" she says, tossing her head and biting the corner of her lower lip very slowly and deliberately. Berkeley Hunt gulps, and is once again barely able to control himself from having a spontaneous emission.

****

Patricia Turbot is lying in a bed. A man's hand reaches over and takes the cigarette from between her fingers. She gets out of bed and puts on a bathrobe.

"Berkeley Hunt ... I don't think that man would notice if I had my big toe stuck up his rear end," remarks Malcolm as he takes a drag from the cigarette. Save for a village idiot, most likely residing in a rural Welsh community, Malcolm, like everyone else in the country, thinks Berkeley Hunt to be a cretin.

"Of course not, Malcolm – not while I've got my whole foot up there," replies Patricia Turbot. She enters the bathroom and continues. "Do you think he's had a lobotomy?"

"I doubt it. You need a brain to have a lobotomy. Anyway, why is it that you always dress so provocatively every time you go to meet Hunt? You know: cleavage and legs. Have you surrendered to that worn-out old cliché by that demented Yank about power being the ultimate aphrodisiac? Or do you have some sort of a thing for him?"

"Are you jealous?" she asks teasingly.

Malcolm fails to pick up on the tease and replies, "Well that's a difficult one. On the one hand, he's hardly Casanova – not with that body and that face. On the other, if you do have a thing for him, I'm wondering what I'm doing wrong."

"Silly boy, of course I don't have a thing for him. But he has a thing for me, and so I play up to it. Your little outburst could have done some real damage otherwise. You should have seen him after you left, poor wee thing. I thought he was going to have an accident in his trousers. By this time next week, if I asked him to run down Whitehall naked, I'm sure he'd do it."

"How do you know he has a thing for you?"

"Men ... Honestly, you're too obsessed with your own gratification to realise that women have had the drop on you for centuries. We understand you better than you understand yourselves. You're predictable and easy to read. If we let you get your leg over twice a week you'll do anything we ask."

Malcolm is slightly deflated.

"I see. It appears I have quite a lot to learn."

"Don't worry. Your next lesson begins right now." She re-enters the bedroom and slips into bed.

****

Mike Hunt is sitting at his desk at the offices of Goldstein Brothers Investment Bank in the City of London. He is having a manicure and his shoes polished and, in spite of the law, is smoking a small cheroot. As a partner, and as head of private and corporate client wealth management at the bank, not only is he very wealthy but he is also extremely influential amongst the financial community and within the organs of various national governments.

Born with an overarching sense of entitlement, his pinched, hawkish face is set in an almost permanent sneer, as though he holds most of the world in complete contempt – which indeed he does. He is typical of most investment bankers, so would rather feed his grandmother to crocodiles, than stand a round of drinks. Mike Hunt is a man who is more than content to sacrifice anything or *anyone* on the altar of his greed and vanity. Like his younger brother, Berkeley, he has a mop of thick blonde hair, but unlike his brother it is coiffed to perfection.

He picks his nose and wipes his finger on the shirt of the shoeshine boy and then straightens his old school tie, which he wears both to intimidate the attendees of lesser public schools and to reinforce his sense of superiority and social order. He picks up his desk phone and dials a number.

Berkeley Hunt is in his office at Number 10. He is having the handcuff removed by a workman with an electric saw when his desk phone rings. He answers it.

"Hello, Humpty," says Mike Hunt.

Berkeley Hunt cringes, as he loathes his childhood nickname. "Hello, Bruiser. Look, I wish you wouldn't call me that. It's only

9

about the thousandth time I've asked you," replies an irritated Berkeley Hunt.

"Calm down and stop being so touchy. What's all that noise in the background?"

"Err ... We've had a bit of an accident with the plumbing."

"What, in your office?"

"Err ... Yes. Anyway, what's up?" Berkeley Hunt gestures the workman to leave (handcuff still attached notwithstanding).

"Just checking to see that you've squashed this absurd tax reform bill."

The manicurist in Mike Hunt's office stands up to leave. Mike Hunt hands her a stack of twenty pound notes and then squeezes her bottom. She giggles and walks out.

"Well, err ... it's a bit of a problem, Bruiser. Pat Turbot and Nick Lafarge are rather stuck on it, and the Opposition are also keen. Can't see how I can stop it. Besides, as a banker, I can't see why you're against it. After all, it makes life for you chaps a lot simpler, surely?"

Barely in control of his temper, Mike Hunt replies, "Do you really think that lawyers, accountants, and bankers could get their cretinous clients to pay exorbitant fees if tax and bureaucracy were simplified? And do you really believe that the tax office want to simplify the tax code?"

"Well, it would make their lives a lot easier."

"Precisely, you halfwit. Do you honestly think that the Permanent Secretary and the rest of 'em want to see their budget cut? How do you think they could preserve their staffing levels if they had almost nothing to do?"

"Err ... Look, Bruiser, I've read through the bill, and my economic advisors tell me that a simpler tax system would benefit everyone and would be a lot more just to the man in the street. Everyone would pay their fair share."

Now roaring, Mike Hunt replies, "Fair share? What makes you think I want to pay my fair share?"

"I don't know why you suggested that I should do this job, if I'm not allowed to do what's right for the British people."

In his rage Mike Hunt stands up and literally kicks the shoeshine boy out of his office.

"If we wanted someone to do what's right for the British people we would have asked the Archbishop of bloody Canterbury to be prime minister, and *not* a clueless idiot!" shouts Mike Hunt.

Summoning up what little courage he has, Berkeley Hunt retorts, "You're not the head boy any more, Bruiser, and I'm no longer your fag. You can't ask me to do the impossible."

"Can't I, indeed? We'll see about that – and you bloody well are my fag! Got some photos of you dressed in baby clothes with a dummy in your mouth. Know the ones I mean?"

Berkeley Hunt goes white.

"You wouldn't. Not those photos …"

"Yes, I would. And, don't forget, I have discretion and control over your trust fund, so bloody well sort it out!" shouts Mike Hunt, slamming down the phone.

Berkeley Hunt puts down the phone, exhales deeply, and hangs his head in his hands. He is both dejected and anxious.

****

Lieutenant Commander Smedley Butler, of the United States Navy, closes the gate to his front garden and makes his way to his car. A man rushes out from his house shouting,

"Hey, you idiot, you almost forgot your pills." Smedley Butler, stops and goes back to retrieve the bottle. The man continues, "Four months on a submarine without these and they'd be putting you in a padded cell."

11

"Sorry," replies a contrite Smedley Butler. He continues to his car, gets in, and drives off.

A short while later his car pulls into the Royal Navy submarine base where he is stationed. He parks his car, gets out, and boards the RN attack submarine HMS *Argo*. Smedley Butler is, as is quite common practice between the Royal Navy and the United States Navy, on an officer exchange programme. Smedley Butler makes his way to his quarters. He is fortunate that he is not required to share them.

He enters his quarters and immediately takes two of his pills. Unbeknownst to anyone, Smedley Butler suffers from claustrophobia, a condition that would instantly disqualify him from a naval career. Naturally, he is not keen to disclose his condition.

There is a knock at the door.

"Come in," says Smedley Butler.

It is the boat's captain.

"Ah, Butler, good to have you back on board," he says.

"Thank you, sir," replies Smedley Butler.

"We have a senator on board, from the Senate Armed Services Committee, and his aide. They are here to evaluate the MRC 414 weapons system, so when you're ready I'd like you to meet me in the weapons room and give them a presentation," says the captain.

"Of course, sir," replies Smedley Butler.

A few minutes later Smedley Butler enters the weapons room. The captain begins the introductions.

"Senator, this is one of your countrymen, Lieutenant Commander Smedley Butler. Commander Butler is here as part of our officer exchange programme with the United States Navy and serves on board as the weapons officer. I have asked him to give you a presentation on MRC 414. Commander Butler, this is Senator Gormmless and his aide, Miss … err …"

"Luvzit. Mona Luvzit," replies the young lady.

"Well, carry on, Butler. We have to be underway by 1600 hours, so I'll have to leave you to it," says the captain, and leaves.

Senator Zachariah Buford Gormmless is chairman of the Senate Oversight Committee for the National Security Commission and vice chairman of the Senate Armed Services Committee. He has much in common with his British counterparts in the House of Lords, being a member of that ever-growing clique of senile old gits who wander aimlessly and absent-mindedly through the corridors of power. He is fortunate that the intelligent and conscientious Mona Luvzit is permanently at hand. He would otherwise have difficulty finding his way out of his bathroom. It's no surprise that it is Mona Luvzit who asks the questions.

"How long has this weapons system been operational?" asks Mona Luvzit.

"Just over a year," replies Smedley Butler.

"Hmm ..." she muses.

"It has been fully tested in both simulations and live firing, Miss Luvzit."

"I see. Can you elaborate on some of the specifications, speed, range, warhead yield, etc.?" she asks.

"Of course. MRC 414, code name Javelin, is a supersonic short range sea-skimming anti-ship missile system. Its maximum velocity is Mach 3.5, about 2,500 mph, depending on temperature. Range is thirty nautical miles. Maximum yield is 2,000 kilograms of high explosive, although we can fit a very low-yield nuclear warhead – say three kilotons. But we don't currently do so," replies Smedley Butler.

"The range seems inadequate for a submarine," she says.

"Not really, and definitely not for this one. The *Argo*-class is currently the most advanced attack submarine in the world, and not even the combined anti-submarine technology of the UK and the US is guaranteed to detect her. But, anyway, it's a trade-off between warhead yield, speed, and range ..."

13

"Look, shall we break for lunch? We can come back and I can elaborate on some of the more technical details then."

"Sure," she replies.

All of them leave the weapons room and head towards the mess.

On entering the mess, and now that the business of government is over, Senator Gormmless is miraculously resurrected from the dead.

"Well, what's for lunch, Captain?"

"Err … It's Commander, actually, sir. I'll go and get a menu," replies Smedley Butler, and makes his way to a vacant table to retrieve a menu. Having spent her entire career as Senator Gormmless's aide, Mona Luvzit has long since grown bored of the inane drivel that passes for his small talk, and looks around to see if she can excuse herself from his company. She is an attractive young woman, and is soon spotted by two young officers who beckon her over.

Smedley Butler returns.

"You don't mind if I go and sit with those gentlemen, Senator? It may prove useful in our fact-finding," she says.

"Of course not, my dear. You go ahead. I'm sure I can entertain the lieutenant on my own," replies Senator Gormmless.

"Err … That should be 'Commander'," says Smedley Butler.

"Yes, of course … Commander, my apologies," replies Senator Gormmless. They both take a seat at a table and order their meal.

Although a cretin with the memory span of a goldfish, Senator Gormmless is proud of his long family history. He hails from a long line of bigoted and racist religious fundamentalist lunatics of precisely the kind that the European Enlightenment was glad to see bugger off to the New World.

"That was a most interesting talk you gave, Commander. Your sonar was quite impressive. Tell me, how long have you been the sonar operator?" asks Senator Gormmless.

"Actually, Senator, I'm the weapons officer, and the talk was about our weapons system," replies Smedley Butler, politely sidestepping the idiocy of the senator's reply.

"Yes … yes, of course. That's what I meant. You know, I was in the navy … Made lieutenant junior grade, served on a flat-top during Vietnam … or was it Korea? I don't suppose it matters. Could never tell one gook from another … Hell, can't even tell the difference between a Guinea and a spic," he says laughing. Their main course arrives.

A few minutes into their main course the senator remarks, "I have to say, Lieut— err, Commander, it's reassuring to know that one of our boys is here showing the Brits how it's done by a *real* naval officer." Smedley Butler winces and squirms slightly, and notices a couple of the other officers turn in their direction.

"I think you'll find, sir, that the Royal Navy is more than capable."

"Well, that's good to know. We don't want to be carrying the Limeys *again* … if it comes to a shooting war," replies the senator. Smedley Butler looks down and places his hand on his forehead to avoid the stares of his comrades. He begins to wish that he was somewhere else.

Dessert arrives.

"So tell me, son, where are you from?" asks the senator.

"San Francisco," replies Smedley Butler.

"San Francisco, eh …? Hmm, Butler … Butler. Are you by any chance one of the Pacific Heights Butlers? Any relation to the late rear admiral Chet Butler?"

"He was my grandfather, sir," replies Smedley Butler.

"Well, well, well. What a coincidence. He was my commanding officer during Vietnam, or was it Korea? Anyway, he was a very fine officer. Quite a ladies' man, as I recall – not that I approve of that sort of thing, of course, the Gormmlesses being a God-fearing Christian family an' all." He takes a bite out of an apple and continues.

"Do you have a wife, son?"

"Err … no, sir, but …"

"Really? A handsome, athletic man like you? I'm surprised women aren't falling at your feet," says the senator.

"No, sir, they're not."

"Every man should have a wife. Can't get ahead in the navy if you don't. Something suspicious about a man who isn't married, don't you agree?" he asks.

"If you say so, Senator."

"My youngest daughter … about your age. Virtuous, if you get my meaning. When you're stateside next time call on her, with my blessing."

"Thank you, Senator, but I'm not so sure. You see—"

"No, no, no, I know what you're thinking. But don't worry, son, there's *never* been a Catholic Gormmless – nor a spineless Quaker in the family, either."

"It's not that, Senator … it's just that I'm already married."

"You said you didn't have a wife," replies the confused Senator, as he takes another bite out of the apple.

"I don't, but…err… I do have a husband."

Senator Gormmless's eyes widen. He turns pale and begins to cough, which turns into a prolonged wheeze. He rasps, "Hu-hu-hus-husband…" His face is beginning to turn blue. Thinking that the senator is choking on the apple, Smedley Butler jumps out of his seat, hauls the senator up, positions himself behind him, and starts to perform the Heimlich manoeuvre.

The senator becomes even more alarmed. Believing that his Puritan virtue is in mortal danger and that the sanctity of his most sacred orifice is about to be violated he gathers all his remaining strength and, reaching down, grabs Smedley Butler's genitals and squeezes as hard as he can. Smedley Butler screams and falls to the floor, writhing in agony and clutching his groin. The senator crashes forward, face first, on to the table.

****

Vladimira Pushkin, the first female president of the Russian Federation, is standing in front of the French windows in her large and very spacious office in the Kremlin. It is late evening in Moscow and she is gazing out on to the illuminated city. In her forties, at six foot she is tall for a woman and svelte of frame. Her high cheekbones, strong chin, green eyes, and raven-black hair are typical of a Slavic beauty. Her beauty, however, belies the cold and ruthless heart that beats beneath her exquisitely shaped breast. Like the black widow spider she is deadlier than the male.

She is a keen horsewoman, and is rather attached to the riding crop that is a permanent fixture in her hand, having once belonged to one of Russia's long list of dictators.

There is a knock on the door. Kronsteen, her personal bodyguard, opens it, and an army general enters the room and approaches her. She waits for a few moments before turning around to face the general. She regards him dispassionately before gesturing for the file he has in his hands. She hands the riding crop to Kronsteen and begins to study the file's contents.

The general is somewhat apprehensive. He has admired her from afar and like many Russian men – and, indeed, some women – he is torn between feelings of lust and dread when in the Russian president's presence.

Vladimira Pushkin continues to study the file while addressing the general.

"I trust all the preparations have now been completed for Operation Grand Slam, and that our military attaché has been fully briefed." There is an air of menace in her voice.

"Indeed," replies the general.

She looks up and fixes the general with an impassive stare.

"I hope so, General. Our gulags are already overflowing. I would not like to think that you would feel claustrophobic, should anything go wrong."

The general begins to visibly perspire.

"I assure you, Madam President, everything will go according to plan," he replies. Saluting, he hurriedly leaves the room.

Day Two

A TV news journalist is speaking to camera inside the White House grounds in Washington DC.

"Well, that concludes the state visit of the Japanese prime minister. This reporter understands that President Hilary Poinswatter has agreed to the Japanese prime minister's request for additional US military bases to be built on the three main Japanese islands and the provision of additional US troops and naval forces.

"Tensions between Japan and China have been rising in recent months, and this is obviously of concern to the current administration. While not wanting to antagonise the Chinese, President Poinswatter needs to show solidarity with the Asia-Pacific allies of the United States – particularly with the growing threat of North Korea, who recently announced the launch of their fourth ballistic missile submarine."

Hilary Poinswatter, the first female president of the United States, has just taken her leave of the Japanese prime minister in the White House and is on her way back to the Oval Office, carrying a large stuffed beaver.

She turns to her aide and says, "Get on the phone to that SOB at Goldstein Brothers. Tell him their payment was late this month and two million short. Remind him that I'm not one of their African puppets and I won't be messed with."

Hilary Poinswatter is a somewhat anodyne, anhedonic individual. She is plain. Some would use the word 'dowdy'. She is a woman whose charm and allure would fail to arouse the passions in a convicted criminal in long-term solitary confinement, even if he had been overdosing on Viagra.

A busty young blonde walks up to her and says, "Oh, Madam President, I'm *so* excited at the opportunity of working right here in the White House. I can't thank you enough."

Hilary Poinswatter nods and smiles coolly at her. The young woman inexplicably curtsies, and then leaves. Hilary Poinswatter enquires of her aide, "Who hired her?"

"Err … I think it was President Poinswatter."

"*I'm* President Poinswatter!" she says, almost barking.

"Err … I mean your husband."

"Is she paid staff?"

"No, she's an intern."

"Well, get rid of her," she says, before entering the Oval Office.

On entering the Oval Office she finds her husband and former president, Jimmy Poinswatter, sitting behind the president's desk playing the saxophone. She puts the stuffed beaver down on her desk, folds her arms, and eyes him disdainfully for a few seconds. She then asks with some annoyance,

"What are you doing in my chair?"

"Just reliving old times, honey," replies Jimmy Poinswatter. He goes back to playing the saxophone. Unlike his wife, Jimmy Poinswatter's numerous conquests of the opposite sex are testament to his charisma and good looks. His prowess is legendary amongst the young socialites of Washington DC. His hair, now quite grey, has added a distinguished dimension to his persona.

She walks around to the other side of the desk and looks at her husband quizzically for a moment, and then says, with surprising composure,

"Monica, you can come out now." A moment later a young brunette emerges from underneath the desk while buttoning up her blouse. She hurriedly leaves the room. Jimmy Poinswatter stands up and zips up his flies.

"You know, I don't really care who is blowing your horn these days, but do you *really* have to do it in my seat?" barks Hilary Poinswatter.

"You know, if *you* were to start blowing my horn again, Hills honey, there wouldn't be any one else *ever* again," he replies, with ill-concealed pretence. He hasn't been attracted to his wife for decades, and knows that she abhors the thought of physical intimacy. His reply is simply a rather poor attempt at placating her.

Hilary Poinswatter is not taken in by his dissembling.

"Really? You know *very* well that, after Everton was born, *that* part of our life had come to an end."

"I know, but I can *still* hope," he lies. "Anyway what's with the stuffed beaver?"

"I don't know. *You* tell me. It's a gift to you from the daughter of the Japanese prime minister. What *exactly* is it that you said to her?" she asks suspiciously.

"Uh ... err ... I think she must have misheard me," he replies.

There is a knock at the door and an aide walks in and tells her it's time for her next scheduled meeting.

****

Poota Bastardo, president of the Argentine nation, is seated in her office reading through a stack of official government documents. A brutally ugly woman, her lack of aesthetic appeal has been exacerbated by numerous cosmetic operations. Her now walrus-like skin would disintegrate even the hardiest of barnacles. She has long since given up trying to attract a spousal companion, male or female, and it is probably the reason why she is indifferent to the very visible moustache that clings to her lip.

Her intercom buzzes and her secretary informs her that Franco Primadonna has arrived. She stands up and shuffles her bulk to the other side of her desk.

Franco Primadonna enters the room carrying a small leather bag. A former World Cup-winning captain of the national football team, Franco Primadonna is now the Minister for Sport. He is quite short, with wiry hair, and sports an earring. His once stocky athletic frame is no more, and after years of excess he now resembles a bloated pot-bellied pig on two legs.

The Argentine president greets him using his nickname.

"El Pibe ..."

"Madrón, ..." he replies. They embrace warmly but platonically.

"How were the negotiations?" she asks.

"They went very well. There will be no problems with transportation, provided you can see to it that our customs officers are fully briefed."

"That won't be a problem. Excellent. What about the quality?" she asks.

"Of the highest grade."

"And the price? I hope you agreed a figure no more than we discussed."

"Better than that, Madrón. I have acquired one ton at a 10 per cent discount."

"Wonderful. I would like to test the merchandise."

"Of course." Franco Primadonna places the leather bag on her desk, unzips it, and removes a clear polythene bag filled with white powder.

They both sample the cocaine using rolled-up Argentine peso notes.

"*Bueno* ... very good. You have done well, El Pibe," she says. She opens a desk drawer that is crammed with US $100 bills and hands Franco Primadonna a large stack. "A bonus for your very good work, El Pibe."

21

"Thank you, Madrón."

"I want you to arrange payment and delivery no later than three days from now. We have very pressing matters to discuss with President Pushkin in Moscow, so I don't want there to be any delays. Now help me with the briefcases."

Franco Primadonna helps her unload a number of aluminium briefcases from a wardrobe and begins to check their contents. Each briefcase is filled with US $100 bills. However, he also discovers one filled with Argentine Pesos.

"Madrón, what is this doing here?"

Poota Bastardo turns to inspect the briefcase.

"Sorry, El Pibe, just put it in the toilet."

"Why?"

"We've run out of toilet paper again, El Pibe. It's ridiculous. We can't even get any for government departments, so what else are we to do?"

****

Back at the White House in Washington DC, the Secretary of the Treasury, the US Attorney General, and a young attractive female staffer are shown into the Oval Office. They all take a seat, including Hilary Poinswatter. Jimmy Poinswatter takes a seat slightly behind his wife and to her right, where he is able to ogle the young attractive female staffer unnoticed. Hilary Poinswatter turns to her husband and asks,

"What are you still doing here?"

"I rather thought I might sit in, if that's OK," he replies. He turns to the two other men. "You don't mind, do you gentlemen?" Both men mumble their assent.

Rather than create a disagreeable scene Hilary Poinswatter simply turns back to her husband and gives him a hard stare.

"Well, let's begin," says Hilary Poinswatter.

The Secretary of the Treasury opens the discussion. "As you know, Madam President, in about four months' time the government will hit the debt ceiling. As you also know, Congress are refusing to budge on raising the ceiling without you significantly diluting your healthcare reforms and removing your proposals for taxing oil and gas."

"Well I'm not going to budge, either, so we're going to have to find some way to avoid, or at least postpone, hitting the debt ceiling," replies Hilary Poinswatter.

Unseen by his wife and the other two men, Jimmy Poinswatter makes a lewd and suggestive gesture to the female staffer. At first the female staffer blushes but, as Jimmy Poinswatter continues to make suggestive gestures, she responds by rolling her tongue around one corner of her top lip. The business discussion continues in the meantime.

"We could cut back significantly on military operations and procurement," suggests the Secretary of the Treasury.

"I've just pledged increased military support to the prime minister of Japan, so that's not an option," replies Hilary Poinswatter, and continues, "How about the Chinese? Surely we can find a few corporations that have committed some serious felonies, and no doubt sanction them heavily. That might bring in some additional revenue."

"That would be a catastrophe, Madam President," says the Secretary of the Treasury.

Meanwhile Jimmy Poinswatter continues to make lewd gestures to the female staffer. The female staffer ups the ante by undoing a couple of buttons on her blouse and begins gently caressing her cleavage.

"Why would it be a catastrophe?" asks Hilary Poinswatter.

"Chinese public and private corporations own about 40 per cent of our national debt between them. If they were of a mind they could cause havoc in our public finances by dumping hundreds of billions

23

of dollars of US government bonds on to the market. The government's cost of borrowing would skyrocket—"

Hilary Poinswatter interrupts. "I can see that, Mr Secretary, but they would lose billions themselves. So what would be the point?"

"In the short term ... Yes, you're right. But the contagion of a collapsing bond market would spread to our equity markets, and would very likely cause a liquidity crisis for our banks. At the moment Chinese banks don't have much exposure to ours. The Chinese also own about 25 per cent of all the equity in publicly traded corporations in the US and have a dollar currency reserve of close to three trillion—"

"I'm sorry, Mr Secretary, you're beginning to lose me," interrupts Hilary Poinswatter once more.

"First of all, unless we were to print money on a scale unprecedented in human history the Chinese could effectively charge extortionate interest rates to our banks, which means the US government as well.

"And second, with their huge currency reserves and a severely depressed equity market, they could buy up US companies at bargain-basement prices. So any losses they may incur initially would be more than compensated for," responds the Secretary of the Treasury.

"I see. So it could be a bad move," says Hilary Poinswatter.

"Yes, Madam President, a *very* bad move, and a bad risk just to find a few billion dollars," replies the Secretary of the Treasury.

"OK. So who else?"

"Don't worry, Hills honey, I'm sure you'll think of *someone* to extort money from," quips Jimmy Poinswatter. Hilary Poinswatter turns to her husband and gives him another *very* hard stare.

The Attorney General begins to speak. "The British—"

"What, extort money from the British *again*? That would only be about the tenth time," interrupts Jimmy Poinswatter, who then bursts out laughing.

Finally losing her patience and temper, Hilary Poinswatter turns to her husband.

"The next time you interrupt I'll have the secret service drag you out of here, so shut up."

Jimmy Poinswatter goes back to exchanging lewd gestures with the female staffer.

"I'm sorry, Attorney General. Please continue," says Hilary Poinswatter. Having lost his train of thought, the Attorney General begins again.

"Aah … the super tanker disaster in the Gulf of Mexico yesterday—"

Hilary Poinswatter interrupts him. "Sorry for the interruption, but that tanker – I believe – is owned by the Exxcreton Corporation, which is our biggest oil company. They're already going to be in deep trouble and have huge financial penalties. That's going to hit US investors very hard. We can't possibly hit them above and beyond what they are already going to pay."

"Not necessarily. Exxcreton may not have to pay a penny," begins the Attorney General. "The tanker was only sold to them two months ago by the British Overseas Oil Corporation (BOOC), and the seaworthiness inspection report was carried out by an associate company. Now, if we can show that the inspection process was negligent in some way – and that there was collusion between the parent company and the associate company – then they, rather than Exxcreton, would be held liable for the spill."

"Could that really be done?" asks Hilary Poinswatter.

"Absolutely. In fact I'm sure we could recover treble the amount from BOOC that we would have been able to recover from Exxcreton," replies the Attorney General.

"How can you be sure?" enquires Hilary Poinswatter.

"No matter how shaky and circumstantial the evidence that we contrive – err, I … I mean *find* – the proceedings will be held in a US court, presided over by a US judge, and the defendant will be a foreign corporation. So I think a guilty verdict would be a slam dunk. Extracting payment won't be a problem, as BOOC have tens of billions of dollars in assets in the US."

"American justice ... don't you just love it?" quips Jimmy Poinswatter once again.

"I'm warning you, Jimmy," snaps Hilary Poinswatter. She continues by concluding, "Very good, Attorney General. I like it. You've earned your pay cheque this month."

"You know, Hills honey, the Brits ain't gonna be very happy. They're still sore at us for screwing them over with Lend-Lease ..." says Jimmy Poinswatter.

"Which is a bonus, and anything that causes problems for Berkeley Hunt is the icing on the cake," says Hilary. "Which reminds me, Attorney General. Have you discovered anything at all about Berkeley Hunt that could initiate criminal proceedings against him in the US?"

"I'm afraid not, Madam President."

"Well, please keep looking," she says.

"What is it with you and Berkeley Hunt? All this anger ... The poor guy's harmless," says Jimmy Poinswatter.

Hilary Poinswatter, almost screeching, shouts, "Harmless! Did you forget what happened at Buckingham Palace last year?"

"Of course not, but don't you think you're overreacting? After all, it was an accident, honey, and kinda funny."

Hilary Poinswatter is now screaming.

"Funny! Did you finally inhale?"

Day Three

Nick Lafarge is standing at the lectern in a conference hall in the UK. He has just finished delivering a speech, to rapturous applause by the conference attendees. He stands for a few moments beaming and basking in the glory of the crowd's adulation.

Nick Lafarge is a thick-set man in his mid fifties. He has a tree trunk of a neck and is rather brutish in appearance. He could quite easily pass for a bouncer in one of Soho's less reputable sex clubs. Despite this he is something of a snappy dresser.

A former stockbroker, Nick Lafarge is a heavy drinker and smoker. He is Eurosceptic, xenophobic, homophobic, and a misogynist. In spite of these attributes, or perhaps because of them, British voters had seen fit to elect him to the House of Commons several years previously. As well as being an MP he is leader of the Federal United Kingdom Union Party, a far-right political party and the newest to be represented in Parliament. FUKUP had found itself in a coalition government with Berkeley Hunt's political party as a consequence of the vagaries of the British electoral process, and Nick Lafarge now finds himself as deputy prime minister.

He steps down from the lectern and is greeted by cheers, applause, and pats on the back. As he makes his way through the aisle he is approached by a well-known journalist from a renowned liberal broadsheet newspaper. He is a chinless, anaemic-looking individual, like most left-leaning liberal hacks. On a point of principle Nick Lafarge feels duty-bound to knee the journalist in the crotch but, with other members of the press gathered, he thinks better of it.

"Mr Lafarge," begins the journalist, in a rather condescending manner, "do you seriously believe that your policy initiatives will gain any traction in Parliament?"

Having been kicked out of a renowned public school, Nick Lafarge's accent is a mixture of his South London scrap merchant family roots and the polished inflection of a private education. He replies in his gravelly, gruff voice,

"Of course, because we have a mandate from the people of this great country to do precisely that. Look, we are supporting wholesale reform of the tax system so that the ordinary people of this country get a fair deal by ensuring that the big corporate interests pay their fair share."

"Yes, Mr Lafarge, but you weren't the ones to originally propose the tax reform bill, and you're not the only party supporting it. Your other initiatives are decidedly xenophobic and homophobic," replies the journalist.

Nick Lafarge throws his hands into the air.

"Look, I am getting tired of these scurrilous accusations. Xenophobic: not one bit. FUKUP is very happy to see Johnny Foreigner on our shores, provided that Johnny Foreigner is prepared to put his hand in his pocket and pay his way. We're not a bloody charity, you know!"

"What about your criticisms of same-sex marriage ...?"

"What criticisms? That's another fabrication by the liberal metropolitan elitist media. In our new manifesto, to be released tomorrow, we will outline our proposals to actively campaign for homosexuals to have their own country. A homeland for homosexuals will mean that they will able to create their own constitution and make their own laws, which will *obviously* sanction same-sex marriage ... and of course there is historical precedent for a gay homeland."

"What precedent?" asks the journalist dubiously, and with more than a little surprise.

"Sodom," replies Nick Lafarge in all seriousness.

"What? Sodom? It probably didn't even exist and, besides, was a city, not a country. But anyway, that's just—"

"A city state, actually, like Athens, with whom they had much in common – you know, the unspeakable vice of the Greeks ... So you can see I've done my research. But you're just splitting hairs. The point is that it will be only the second time in history that a nation will have been reborn. Coincidentally, it will also be in the Middle East, and this time thanks to FUKUP."

"Well, I must say, it *really* is quite incredible."

"Thank you," replies Nick Lafarge, failing to detect the withering sarcasm in the journalist's voice.

"No, what I *mean* is ... It is quite incredible that the British people have been as gullible and as stupid as they have, to vote you into office," says the journalist, with unmistakable contempt.

Annoyed by the affront, Nick Lafarge retorts, "I think I've answered all your questions. Now bugger off," as he storms off. He turns to two of his heavily built party lackeys and says, "When the conference is over, be discreet and take that pillock round the back. Don't break anything, but give him a good kicking."

****

Malcolm is pouring himself a drink while Patricia Turbot, first minister of Scotland, dries herself off from her shower. They are in Patricia Turbot's Westminster flat.

"Why don't you get a divorce?" asks Malcolm.

"A divorce? What on earth for?" replies Patricia Turbot.

"I rather thought we could get married," says Malcolm, a touch of surprise laced into his voice.

29

"Married? Darling, you're very sweet and a fantastic lover, but how would we manage?" replies Patricia Turbot.

"Well, with your salary as first minister and mine as your aide, we'd easily get by," says Malcolm.

"Get by? Malcolm, do you think I just want to *get by*? Your tailored suits and handmade shoes ... who pays for them? Me, and who do you think pays for me and my luxuries? Reggie," she replies, referring to her husband.

"I can do without the suits and the shoes. I only bother wearing them to please you. Besides, what's money got to do with anything?" he asks.

"I'm not going to be the first minister *forever*, Malcolm, which means you're not going to be the first minister's aide forever—"

"That doesn't matter. We'll manage. Love always finds a way," he interrupts confidently, if somewhat naively.

"Grow up, Malcolm. Money matters a *very* great deal. Do you really think I want to give up our houses in Marbella and Barbados to go and live with you on a housing estate in Glasgow? If I get a divorce there'll be no settlement, no maintenance payments for me. I'll have nothing," she replies angrily.

"Why do you care about any of that? We're socialists, remember. You know, freeing ourselves from the oppressive yoke of English capitalism and redistributing wealth equally to all Scotsman ... or had you forgotten that?" says Malcolm.

"That's very funny, Malcolm, considering it was a Scot who practically invented capitalism," she replies.

"I'm serious. We were elected to bring people out of poverty in an independent country, and with our oil reserves we can do precisely that," he retorts.

She laughs.

"Oh, be serious. You don't really want to turn Scotland into a workers' paradise, do you? As for independence, that's to be avoided at all costs."

"What! Are you winding me up? Is that a joke?"

"Of course not. If you think our economic problems are bad now, then just wait and see what our economy would look like if we were independent. Without our own currency – not that we could afford to buy the foreign currency reserves to have one – it would be a disaster. We would be at the mercy of and subject to the whims of English monetary and fiscal policy.

"Of course we could join the euro, but as that's about to collapse it would be an even bigger disaster. Oh, yes, and joining the European Community ... Well, that's an extra two billion pounds we'd have to find every year – assuming someone doesn't block our entry, that is," she replies.

"Our oil reserves will get us through, surely?"

"What oil reserves? What little there is can't be taxed any more. The oil companies wouldn't stand for it. They'd up sticks and disappear. And, besides, closing down the existing platforms will cost billions in tax relief, which the Scottish people will have to find on their own if we're independent," she replies.

"Why are we campaigning for independence if our prospects are so bad ? And why the hell do you keep asking Hunt for a referendum if you don't believe in a free and independent Scotland?" Malcolm asks, almost shouting the question.

"The more the English believe we want to be free, the more they bend over backwards to hold on to us. All the concessions and money we've wrung out of them over the decades wouldn't have happened if we didn't keep threatening to walk away," she replies.

"Are you telling me we've been conning the people and lying to our supporters all these years?" he asks, disbelievingly.

"The people ... ha! People will believe anything if you come up with a convincing enough narrative. And no one is more gullible or susceptible to a good yarn than a Scotsman with an inferiority complex and more testosterone than brain cells. I'm sure you haven't forgotten how they threw themselves willingly on the English bayonets at Culloden, only for the survivors to be shot to pieces. Independence was the best narrative of all. The people bought it and are still buying it, and in the end they've been better off for it. So what harm has been done?" she replies, shrugging her shoulders innocently.

"The oldest delusion in politics: rationalising dishonesty in the supposed service of the greater good. It's the same sort of dissembling spouted by Teflon Tony after he took us to war in the Middle East. He'd be proud of you," replies Malcolm, now quite bitter and angry.

"Don't get holier-than-thou with me, Malcolm. You're the one sleeping with another man's wife," she retorts.

"And you are equally guilty in that regard. Tell me, what would Reggie do if he knew about us?" he replies grimly.

"Guilty?" she laughs. "I don't think so. You know, until today I thought that you suspected but were keeping quiet because you too were thrilled, but obviously you don't know."

"Suspected what? And what don't I know?"

"Why do you think you come on holiday with Reggie and me? Because Reggie enjoys watching our performances and I enjoy Reggie watching. I'm sure that when he watches the DVD of today's performance he'll be very thrilled."

Malcolm splutters into his drink.

"Besides," she continues, "the poor darling can't make wee Jimmy stand to attention anymore."

****

HMS *Argo* is sailing submerged, somewhere in the North Atlantic. She is heading towards the South Atlantic to relieve her sister ship HMS *Ariadne*, who is on patrol there.

Smedley Butler is lying on his bunk in his quarters. Even after two days he needs to continue pressing an ice pack to his groin. He is still in some pain from Senator Gormmless's seemingly unprovoked attack. There is a knock on his door.

"Come in," he says weakly. The captain enters, and Smedley Butler tries to stand up.

"No, no, you stay where you are, Butler," says the captain. "How are you feeling? How are your ... err ... um ... err ..."

"My privates, sir?"

"Err ... yes."

"Still rather sore. The doc has given me some quite strong painkillers, which help," replies Smedley Butler.

"Good. Well, he tells me that you'll make a full recovery and will probably be ready for light duties quite soon. You could've been put ashore, you know, Butler. I'm sure we would have managed without you," says the captain.

"I know, sir, but I'll be OK in a few days and I didn't want to let the other guys down. Is there any news about the senator?" asks Smedley Butler.

"Actually, that's why I'm here. CinC Fleet sent through the post-mortem report a couple of hours ago. I asked the doc to look through it and explain what it means," says the captain.

"Did he choke to death?" asks Smedley Butler.

"That's the puzzling thing about it. It appears that he had a brain aneurysm brought on by an apoplectic fit. So it would seem that he suffered some sort of shock to the system. Quite unusual, I'm told. I don't like to ask, Butler, but did you say anything that could have ... well ... discomfited him in any way?" asks the captain.

"I don't think so, sir," replies Smedley Butler.

"Do you recall what you were talking about?" asks the captain.

"Very well, actually. Just before he had his err ... episode, we were discussing my grandfather. It seems that the senator served under his command. I told him I was married, and boom! That's when he seemed to start choking."

"Which, it transpires, he wasn't. Most peculiar. Can't see how that could have set him off. So the only explanation as to why he decided to grab hold of your tackle is some sort of involuntary spasm as a result of the fit he was experiencing, because I can't imagine what he thought you were trying to do to him otherwise," says the captain, mystified.

Smedley Butler is struck by the sudden realisation of *exactly* what the late senator thought he was trying to do to him.

"Well, perhaps … err … no … no … it's nothing," says Smedley Butler.

"Are you sure?" asks the captain.

"Absolutely," replies Smedley Butler.

"Unfortunate business, but we can't be crying over spilt milk. Don't feel too bad, Butler, and don't blame yourself. It wasn't your fault," says the captain.

"Err … no sir, thank you," replies Smedley Butler.

The captain leaves. Smedley Butler lies back down on his bunk and continues to nurse his groin.

Day Six

Admiral Busone Fellatcio, chief of staff of the armed forces of Argentina, is gazing through the window of his office in Buenos Aires. Like most high-ranking South American military officers, his vast array of medals almost completely obscures his uniform. A career officer, he is Argentina's most highly decorated veteran.

It was while on a classified special forces operation in Chilean Tierra del Fuego that the young Lieutenant Fellatcio earned Argentina's highest award for bravery. His troop accidentally stumbled on a colony of penguins which, on becoming distressed, raised the alarm to the presence of the troops. Their operation now compromised, Lieutenant Fellatcio's men were forced to engage in combat. Heavily outnumbered and armed only with automatic weapons, grenades, and flamethrowers, Fellatcio's men fought their way valiantly to freedom for several hours. Although they too fought doggedly and bravely, the penguins proved no match for the highly trained soldiers. Hundreds were slaughtered during the battle.

In his reverie Admiral Fellatcio smiles at the memory of his greatest personal triumph.

He is jolted from his daydreaming by his intercom buzzing.

"The Russian military attaché is here for his appointment, Admiral," says his secretary.

The Russian military attaché is shown in.

"Good morning, Colonel," says Admiral Fellatcio, gesturing him to take a seat.

"Good morning, Admiral," replies the Russian military attaché.

"What can I do for you?" asks the admiral.

The colonel opens his briefcase, extracts an envelope, and passes it to the admiral. The admiral opens the envelope and begins to study the enclosed photographs.

While pointing to a photograph the colonel begins. "I believe that young man's ambition is to get very high up in navy personnel … By the look of ecstasy on your face I would say that he has."

"I'm disappointed in you, Colonel. This isn't Russia. We're far more open-minded about such things. Besides, I would've thought by now you'd be aware of this long-standing Argentine naval tradition. And, clearly, you are not aware of the benefits to morale of such friendships. So as some sort of threat this has absolutely no currency," replies the admiral, waving the photographs in the air before throwing them back at the colonel.

"Yes … yes, I thought you'd say something like that. In spite of my efforts to dissuade them of the futility of such a tactic my superiors overruled me. They have no real understanding of the culture down here, you see.

"However, this *does* have currency, I believe," says the colonel, passing the admiral another envelope. The admiral opens the envelope and begins to examine the documents contained therein.

The colonel, now more confidently, says, "The military procurement budget between our two countries. As you can see, we have irrefutable evidence that you have been … aah … as the Americans would say, 'skimming off the top'. I'm sure President Bastardo would be particularly aggrieved, as I am certain that you have not been giving her a cut. And, of course, if this were to be made public, you would find yourself disgraced and serving a very long prison sentence."

"All right, Colonel, what do want?" replies the admiral.

"While she is in Moscow you will replace her presidential guard with these men," says the colonel, handing over a list to the admiral.

"Is that it?"

"Far from it. On the day before President Bastardo's return from Moscow you are to place the army on a heightened state of alert. You are to double the security around the Parliament building, the presidential palace, and this list of key infrastructure and communication sites around the country. A battalion of commandos from Sverdlovsk will be arriving in thirty-six hours. You will see to it that they are billeted at these various strategic sites around the capital," replies the colonel, handing him two more lists.

"What is the purpose of all of this?" asks the admiral.

"That is not your concern for the present, Admiral. On President Bastardo's return from Moscow you will receive further instructions, which we expect to be carried out to the letter. Needless to say, this matter is strictly confidential," replies the colonel.

"What if I were to tell you to go to hell, Colonel?"

"Then in ten minutes the police with the Attorney General will be here to arrest and charge you with fraud, corruption, and embezzling the Russian Federation. Even if, by some miracle, you survive those consequences, you will not be so fortunate when it comes to the Russian government. We have little tolerance for those who ... offend us," replies the colonel menacingly.

Admiral Fellatcio stares coldly at the colonel. He realises that the battle is lost.

****

Nick Lafarge steps out of a minibus. He is accompanied by an entourage of FUKUP members – a pretty rum lot, mostly of the skinhead and neo-fascist variety. They enter a public house, order and collect their drinks, and return to the street, where they can all smoke.

"Right, lads, we'll have a few pints here. Then it's off to Whitehall to meet my old mate, Vice President Schwarzenkopf.

Don't forget we're in Soho, so keep your backs to the wall, your shirts tucked in, and run at the first smell of a fruit tea," jokes Nick Lafarge. His entourage burst out laughing at his supposed pithy humour.

As is their custom, indeed their political philosophy, the FUKUP members spend the next half-hour harassing, jostling, and generally intimidating every male who passes them by who does not measure up to their standard of virility and masculinity.

Having consumed several dozen pints of beer between them, Lafarge decides it's time to leave, and shouts, "Right, boys, off we go." They all begin to file into the minibus. "Steady, lads, watch out for bandits on your six as you get in," Nick Lafarge slurs drunkenly. His entourage laugh dutifully. The minibus moves off and heads towards Whitehall.

The minibus stops outside of a well-known public house on Whitehall. Lafarge and his crew stumble out and make their way inside the pub. Nick Lafarge spots his old friend Vice President Schwarzenkopf standing at the bar. He is flanked by his secret service bodyguards.

Arnold Schwarzenkopf is the vice president of the United States of America and a former Hollywood movie actor. He himself barely takes the latter label seriously, like everyone else. He is a big man of muscular build. A one-time political mentor to Nick Lafarge, they are now firm friends.

"Arnie … Good to see you again," says Nick Lafarge, his arms outstretched.

"And you, Nick. How's your wife and my kids?" jokes Vice President Schwarzenkopf in his strong Germanic accent.

"Unfortunately the wife's still alive and the kids are halfwits," replies Nick Lafarge. Both men laugh and slap each other on the back.

Bob Boner, a humourless, misanthropic, and world-class sanctimonious arsehole, has been following Nick Lafarge for a few days. They have a mutual loathing, mostly due to their diametrically opposing political views on the merits of the European Community. Boner is a member of that well-known left-wing liberal association of British and American multi-millionaire actors, pop stars, comedians, and authors, who devote part of their time lecturing and berating the hard-pressed middle and working classes for not doing enough to help the less fortunate, while spending much of the rest of their time in finding ways to avoid paying tax.

Boner has followed Lafarge to exact revenge for the deputy prime minister deliberately ramming his boat on the River Thames while campaigning on the European Community referendum. He enters the pub with a group of his heavies. He is a former second-rate movie actor, whose ability and repertoire were widely regarded by critics as utter crap.

Subsequently he has become celebrated for his political activism and his charity work. The latter has made him rather wealthy, as he had negotiated a cut of 20 per cent of all donations. Renowned for railing against the political establishment, he is famed for his pious proselytising on subjects ranging from legalising narcotics to the iniquities of social inequality and the decadence of rampant capitalism – for which, inexplicably, he had been awarded an MBE.

He turns to one of his heavies, hands him his gold Rolex watch, and instructs him to go outside to keep an eye on the Bentley. And then, approaching Nick Lafarge from the rear, he shouts, "You've been asking for this for a long time, Lafarge."

Nick Lafarge turns around and ducks just in time as Bob Boner throws a punch at him. The punch lands squarely on the jaw of Arnold Schwarzenkopf. At first Schwarzenkopf is stunned, and then he growls menacingly. His secret service protection detail springs into action at once.

Now somewhat perplexed, Bob Boner mutters, "Oh, bugger …"

"What happens to *bad* boys who don't eat their vegetables?" says Penny menacingly as she removes the blindfold from Berkeley Hunt, who is handcuffed to her bed. Dressed in her dominatrix leathers, she is holding a large carrot and waving it threateningly. Berkeley Hunt trembles, anticipating the pleasures to come.

"They get severely punished," he replies, his voice quivering, as he is barely able to control his excitement.

For a few moments his imagination works overtime, and it is Patricia Turbot who he sees, dressed as a dominatrix, who is about to administer punishment. It is her voice he hears.

"And *where* do they get severely punished?" snarls Patricia Turbot.

Half an hour later, Berkeley Hunt, wincing and feeling around his rear end, says, "Penny dear, perhaps next time try not to push quite so hard …"

Now feeling considerably more relieved, relaxed, and de-stressed, Berkeley Hunt makes himself comfortable on the bed next to Penny. They begin to watch a movie on the TV. Penny is eating a carrot. They are both silent for a few moments.

"Berkeley?"

"Yes?"

"Can I ask you a question?"

"Well, as long as it's not about politics. Couldn't help you there, I'm afraid," he laughs.

"No, silly … You know I'm doing this degree in sociology and psychology, don't you?

"Vaguely."

"Well, my tutor thought it would be a good idea, for my thesis, to explore the reasons as to why my punters are partial to … err … well…"

"To what?"

"You *know*," she says, trying not to state the bleeding obvious.

"Oh. Your services, you mean. Hold on a mo … You mean your tutor knows what you do for a living?"

"Of course he does. He's one of my punters. Anyway, it will all be very secret, so you don't have to worry. So what do you say?"

"Well, I don't suppose it matters. If I don't stop the tax reform bill it'll all come out anyway."

"What do you mean?" she asks.

"Oh, nothing," he says wearily. "Just thinking out loud. Anyway, what do you want to know?"

"Well, how did you first discover that you like to be … well … punished … shall we say?" she asks, picking up a pen and notebook.

"When I was a sprog. You see, Bruiser and I were always getting into trouble. The thing is … it was only ever me who got caught. He seemed to get away with everything. Still does. He actually set fire to the house, and it was me who got blamed for it. So it was only ever me who got punished, and it was always Nanny who punished me.

"But it was at prep school that I really started enjoying being thrashed. You see, I could never decline the Latin nouns nor conjugate the verbs … or was it the other way round? Anyway, the Latin master ended up tiring himself out, thrashing me day after day. By the end of every term he was totally knackered."

After putting down her pen and notebook, Penny replies, "Well, thank you, Berkeley, that was very helpful." They both resume watching the TV for a few minutes.

"Can I ask you another question, Berkeley?"

"Very well. Go on, then. I should be charging you," he laughs.

"How did you get to be prime minister? I sort of can't work out how it all happened."

"You're not the only one. Something of a mystery to me, as well. You remember the last PM died of a heart attack?

"Of course."

"Shame, really. She was a rather decent old girl. Quite strict, wouldn't take any nonsense from anyone. Sort of reminded me of Nanny." Berkeley Hunt shudders at the thought of the comparison.

"Well, as you know I was Foreign Secretary at the time. Didn't think I was in with a shout of the top spot, and was glad … didn't want it. Anyway it looked as though the Chancellor was going to get the job, but he got nicked for tax evasion and insider dealing—"

"Why didn't you want to be prime minister?" interrupts Penny. "Sounds like a cushy job to me."

"Far from it. You have to meet the most awful people: shifty businessmen who want a knighthood for making themselves billions while exploiting their workers and ripping off their pension funds, pop singers who can't sing, actors who can't act, comedians who aren't funny, and sportsmen who'd rather be celebrities, because it's too much hard work being a sportsman. They're all after the same thing: a knighthood, a peerage, or something, because they've given a few quid that they won't miss to some charity that they pretend to care about." He is silent and unusually reflective for a few moments.

"Well, go on, Berkeley. You haven't finished," says Penny impatiently.

"What? … Oh, yes. So one Sunday I was just minding my own business at home when Bruiser turns up with the party chairman. Well, the party chairman was concerned that another load of skeletons could fall out of the party closet if anyone of the more obvious candidates were to put themselves forward.

"Bruiser said that the party needed someone without any obvious political views, opinions, or any real motivation to change anything, or just … any real motivation at all. Between them they decided that I was the man for the job. I wasn't sure whether to be insulted or flattered, and didn't like the idea anyway."

"But didn't you think you might be able to do some real good for the people?"

42

"I did at the beginning, but am not sure now. But anyway, Bruiser threatened to tie up my trust fund for years if I didn't do it, so I would pretty much be broke. And to be honest, Penny dear ... that's why I took the job. I know I'm not the brightest bulb on the Christmas tree but even I've realised that whatever you try to do for the better, they always seem to have you outnumbered."

His mobile phone rings. He answers it and asks, "Yes, Sir Percy, what is it? ... He what? ... No, no, he can rot there till tomorrow ... Why? Because in a couple of hours that old bag in the Oval Office will be bashing my ears ... I'm sure you'll think of something, Sir Percy." He hangs up.

"Everything all right, Berkeley?" asks Penny.

"No, it bloody well isn't. Lafarge has caused a stink."

****

A few hours previously...

A police superintendent – *the* most obtuse policeman in the history of policing, a man whose cognitive abilities would rival those of a comatose lemming – is questioning Arnold Schwarzenkopf, Nick Lafarge, and Bob Boner. All of them have torn clothing and various cuts and bruises resulting from the mass brawl inadvertently started by Bob Boner. All three are handcuffed and Arnold Schwarzenkopf's secret service bodyguards are lying face down on the pavement, hands on heads, guarded by two armed policemen.

"You do realise that carrying firearms in the United Kingdom is a criminal offence?" The superintendent addresses the question to Arnold Schwarzenkopf.

"They are my secret service protection detail," shouts Arnold Schwarzenkopf.

"And who are you?" queries the superintendent.

"I am the vice president of the United States!" shouts Arnold Schwarzenkopf, even more loudly.

"You sound like a Kraut," replies the superintendent.

Arnold Schwarzenkopf, who is now bellowing, shouts, "I'm Austrian, you fool!"

"You just said you were an American."

"What kind of an imbecile are you?" Arnold Schwarzenkopf bellows once more.

"That's twice you've insulted me. It's an offence to do so to a police officer, but as you're *obviously* ...a Kraut, I'll let it go."

Nick Lafarge, who is now also losing his temper, says, "Listen to me, you stupid pleb. I'm—"

"Pleb? That's a French insult, isn't it, Dimbleby?" enquires the superintendent. Clearly he is a man destined to become Commissioner of The Metropolitan Police.

Dimbleby, his marginally less obtuse younger colleague, replies, "Err ... No, sir, it's Ancient Greek." Dimbleby is undoubtedly a classics scholar in the making.

"Now, look here. I'm the deputy prime minister, and I'm telling you—"

Lafarge is interrupted once more by the superintendent. "Are you telling me that the vice president of the United States and the deputy prime minister are causing an affray, criminal damage, and actual bodily harm in a London pub? What sort of fool do you take me for?"

"Sir, this could be some sort of lookalikes gig that went a bit pear-shaped. They do look like who they say they are," interjects Dimbleby.

"You might have been right, Dimbleby, except lookalikes don't carry firearms." On turning to Bob Boner he says, "Well, Boner, what's really going on here?"

"How do you know that's Bob Boner, sir?" asks Dimbleby.

"Because I've nicked him before," replies the superintendent.

After realising, like everyone else, that the superintendent is a moron, and while sensing an opportunity to cause trouble and perhaps save himself, Bob Boner replies, "You're right, superintendent. Those two aren't who they say they are. The word on the street was that a big German man who was posing as the US vice president, but who was actually a well-known drug smuggler, was over here making a big deal with, err … that man." He says, while pointing to Nick Lafarge.

"What?" exclaim Nick Lafarge and Arnold Schwarzenkopf simultaneously.

"When I and my group tried to break up their nefarious activity they and their goons attacked us, and we were forced to defend ourselves," continues Bob Boner.

"This is ridiculous!" shouts Nick Lafarge.

"Really? Well it sounds a lot more believable to me," replies the superintendent.

"I want to see the US ambassador now," screams Arnold Schwarzenkopf.

"I don't think so, sir, " says the superintendent and then pointing to Nick Lafarge and Arnold Schwarzenkopf says, "Dimbleby, take those two into custody. Mr Boner, I want you to come to the station and make a formal identification and statement. We can go in my car."

Nick Lafarge and Arnold Schwarzenkopf are dragged away kicking and screaming by several police officers. They hurl abuse and curses at Bob Boner, who turns to them, smiles, and offers them a two-fingered salute.

****

"Berkeley, 'Lafarge' doesn't sound like an English name, does it?" says Penny.

"It isn't. It's French, but I doubt that bugger can speak French. He can barely speak English," says Berkeley Hunt, blowing out his cheeks in exasperation.

45

"Why did you get into politics if you're always so stressed out?" asks Penny.

"Penny dear, if you're going to ask me any more questions I'll expect a discount next time," he replies, somewhat irritably.

There is a long pause.

"Well, are you going to tell me or not?" she asks. Berkeley Hunt remains obstinately silent.

"Berkeley, if you don't tell me you know what's going to happen to you, don't you?" she says, glaring at him.

"Threatening to thrash me is not much of a threat, is it?"

"Actually, Berkeley, I was going to threaten *never* to thrash you *again*, and I'll see to it that none of the other girls in this town do either. What do you say to that? Ha!"

Rather petulantly and tersely, Berkeley says, "Oh, very well ... if you must know..."

He continues, squirming with embarrassment, "The truth of the matter is ... I ... I couldn't get a proper job, so I had no choice. I did ask Bruiser if he could get me a job at his bank, but he said I was unsuitable."

"Why?"

"He said that banking was all about honesty, integrity, and doing the right thing, and that ..."

"But that's silly. You're one of the nicest, most trustworthy people I know."

"What he meant, Penny dearest, was that I had *too much* honesty and integrity, and would end up doing the right thing by the client. No bank in their right mind would take me on, let alone Goldstein Brothers. So through his party contacts he arranged for me to be selected as the party candidate in a safe seat."

While reflecting on both brothers, she replies, "Yes ... yes. I can see you're not like him at all."

"You know Bruiser?" he replies, more than a little surprised.

"Oh, yes, and he does have a higher tolerance for pain than you as well," she replies, pointing towards her dressing table.

Berkeley Hunt's eyes widen as his gaze is directed towards a large, prickly cactus on the tabletop.

His mobile phone rings.

"Hello, Humpty," says Mike Hunt. Berkeley Hunt is now too weary even to protest at the use of his nickname.

"Err … look, Bruiser, I haven't found a way to scotch—"

"Don't worry about that," interrupts Mike Hunt. "I phoned to apologise. Sorry about the other day — went over the top, overreacted … been stressed out at work recently … having a massage to ease the strain. Don't want to upset you. We are brothers, after all," says Mike Hunt.

Mike Hunt cares not one jot about being Berkeley Hunt's brother. But, having calmed down, he realises that his brother is worth more to him as prime minister than not. He continues by saying, "Now, look, I can help put an end to this ridiculous tax reform nonsense."

"Look, Bruiser, don't you think that we should allow Parliam—?"

"Now, now, Humpty, just do as you're told. You know I'm right. I *really* wouldn't want to use those photos, and besides I'm only doing what's best for your premiership."

Not wanting to be publicly ridiculed, and now quite inured to the ravages and brutality of both his brother and politics in general, Berkeley Hunt surrenders to the inevitable.

"Well, what do you propose?" he asks wearily.

Mike Hunt turns over on to his back and nods to the masseuse.

"Hold on a minute. I'm just being finished off." A series of groans, moans, and a long sigh of relief are heard by a puzzled and rather discomfited Berkeley Hunt.

"That's better. Sorry about that," says Mike Hunt. "Where were we? Ah yes, tax reform. A two-pronged attack.

"A very useful piece of information came my way yesterday. I'll send it along to Number 10 shortly, with another file I've had for some time. Once you read the contents even you will know what to do. That's the first prong.

"The second prong will kick tax reform into the long grass for at least a decade. What you do is this. You propose to your Cabinet and Parliament that a comprehensive review is to be undertaken by three or four of the leading think tanks in the field. I suggest using the Institute for Fiscal Analysis, the Centre of Economic Policy Studies, and the Institute of Economic Policy Research—"

Berkeley Hunt interrupts. "But how can you be certain that they'll come up with the conclusion you want?"

"Because all three are funded by individuals and corporations that hold the same views as me. There isn't a hope in hell that any of them will support any sort of change in tax law, and it will take a couple of years to conduct the review. Problem solved," replies his brother.

"Well, if you say so."

"I do indeed. Well, got to go … Oh, yes, give my regards to Penny."

Day Seven

Berkeley Hunt and the Cabinet Secretary, Sir Percy Talleewacker, are watching the TV news in the prime minister's office. Nick Lafarge and Arnold Schwarzenkopf are shown being led into the back of a police van as the news commentator recounts the circumstances of the previous day's pub brawl.

"Right, Sir Percy, you better phone the plod and tell them to release Lafarge."

"Very well, Prime Minister," replies Sir Percy.

Just as he is about to leave the room another news item is being reported. Sir Percy stops and continues to watch the report. The news commentator announces the state visit of Poota Bastardo, president of the Argentine nation, and Franco Primadonna to the Russian Federation. Footage shows them being greeted by Russian dignitaries in Moscow.

"What's that woman up to?" asks Berkeley Hunt.

"Which one?" replies Sir Percy.

"Bastardo."

"She's gone there with her begging bowl. After the mess she's made of their economy she needs to buy some time. Don't forget they're in deep hock to the Russians. And, because of that, it's more worrying to think about what that she-devil Pushkin has got up her sleeve."

"What do you mean, Sir Percy?"

49

"It's not just the loans and the bailouts. It's the substantial military aid and the training that the Russians have been providing to Argentina, mostly gratis. Pushkin will want her pound of flesh at some point," he says sombrely.

****

Poota Bastardo and Franco Primadonna are shown into Vladimira Pushkin's office in the Kremlin. Kronsteen, her ever-present bodyguard, escorts them to their seats in front of Pushkin's desk.

As well as her riding crop Vladimira Pushkin's other prized possession is her champion-bred Siberian cat, Kropotkin, who sleeps purring on her lap. She caresses it with long, slow, measured strokes as Poota Bastardo and Franco Primadonna look on. She remains silent for a few moments, gazing out of the windows. Even though Bastardo and Primadonna are hardened South American drug smugglers both feel somewhat unsettled by the silence.

The Russian president turns to her guests and her face is instantly transformed into a warm and welcoming smile, which puts her visitors at ease, while her cold, calculating brain assesses their mettle.

"It is such a pleasure to finally meet you, dear Poota," begins Vladimira Pushkin. Poota Bastardo is slightly irritated by the use of her first name. She is not used to such disregard for protocol, even from another head of state.

"And, of course, the legendary Franco Primadonna. How could anyone forget the sheer genius of that first goal you scored against England in the World Cup? It so typified the character of your nation," concludes the Russian president.

Poota Bastardo translates for the benefit of Primadonna, who smiles and nods in acknowledgement.

"Likewise, Madam President. We were most grateful for your invitation, and are delighted to be here," replies Poota Bastardo.

50

"So how can the peoples of the Russian Federation be of assistance to you, my dear Poota?" asks Vladimira Pushkin. Poota Bastardo is relieved by the genial tone of her voice. Having borrowed billions of dollars from the Russians, which Argentina cannot pay back, Poota Bastardo had expected a more reproving riposte.

She replies, "Naturally, we are very grateful for your economic assistance, and indeed your support for our military, over the last few years. The economic improvements that I had outlined to you through our Ministry of Finance two years ago, however, have not materialised. I was hoping that you would consider rescheduling our loan repayments and perhaps deferring our interest payments for a further two years."

"I do not see that as being a problem," replies Vladimira Pushkin earnestly. Surprised, Poota Bastardo replies, "Really? That is unexpectedly generous of you ... err, I mean ..."

"We are allies, my dear Poota, if not formally then certainly in spirit. Anything to assist a dear friend in our common cause can only be to the benefit of both our nations.

"But please forgive me ... I have been most discourteous. I almost forgot. I have planned a wonderful surprise for you both as a gesture of our enduring friendship." She gestures them towards the French windows, which Kronsteen opens. Kropotkin, her cat, now awake, jumps down from her lap and follows the two South Americans as they make their way towards the French windows and outside balcony.

Kronsteen waits beside the windows. He is a big, broad man of six foot six. A veteran of numerous covert combat operations, he has never been defeated in hand-to-hand combat, and so acquired the nickname of 'God' as a mark of respect by his comrades in his special forces regiment. He has long since lost count of the number of men he has killed, and those are just the ones with his bare hands.

51

Franco Primadonna is more than a foot shorter than the big man, and he looks up nervously into Kronsteen's expressionless face as he passes him and steps out on to the balcony.

The South Americans stare down into the courtyard below, but are puzzled as to what the surprise might be. In a lightning move Kronsteen grabs Franco Primadonna by the back of his trouser belt and hurls him over the balcony on to the concrete, seventy feet below. He is killed instantly. It is perhaps something less than justice for the thousands of victims of his iniquitous trade. Poota Bastardo stares at the growing pool of blood that envelopes his body. And then, turning to Kronsteen, she lets out a petrified shriek.

Kronsteen's normally impassive face breaks out into a broad grin. Then laughing he says, "The hand of God," while holding up his hand and continuing to laugh. Poota Bastardo turns and runs as fast as she can, which isn't very fast, towards the door. Kropotkin chases after her and places himself between her and the door. Hissing, he bears his fangs, and claws at the air in front of her. Alarmed once more, she stops. In a few short steps Kronsteen has caught up with her.

"Kropotkin … Here, now," shouts Vladimira Pushkin. Still hissing, bearing his fangs, and continuing to eye Poota Bastardo malevolently, Kropotkin moves off towards his mistress. Poota Bastardo turns to the Russian president.

"Wh-wh-why?" she screams fearfully.

"Calm yourself, dear Poota. You are in no danger. Come, sit down," says Vladimira Pushkin, gesturing her back to her seat. Poota Bastardo remains hesitant.

"My dear Poota, it would have been just as easy for Kronsteen to toss you over the balcony too. Please sit."

Unsurely, Poota Bastardo shuffles her way back to her chair, shepherded by Kronsteen.

"Kronsteen, some brandy for our guest," says the Russian president. Kronsteen walks to the drinks cabinet and pours out an extra-large measure of the liquid and places it in front of Poota Bastardo. She gulps half of it down in one go.

Vladimira Pushkin continues by explaining the situation to Poota.

"Your recently departed minister was about to betray you to Interpol and the US Drug Enforcement Bureau on your stopover in Paris. He was going to provide irrefutable evidence concerning your narcotics operation and details of where all of the funds you have accumulated are hidden. In exchange he was to be granted immunity from prosecution, given political asylum, and allowed to keep most of the money he himself had acquired in assisting you in your venture."

The Argentine president looks aghast.

"I do not believe it. How do you know this?" she replies incredulously.

"I have my own agents in Interpol and the DEB and, as you will see, in the British Establishment. Here," she says, tossing a file over to Poota Bastardo, who opens it and studies its contents for a few minutes.

"I don't believe it. He was *really* going to do it?" says Poota Bastardo on looking up. "I've known him since we were children. After all I've done for him, and all the money he's made. His family will pay dearly for his deception."

"Yes, it's difficult to know who to trust these days," says the Russian president, eying Poota Bastardo like a cobra eying a gerbil.

"Fortunately, my agents discovered his deception and disloyalty some months ago. Equally fortunately, Primadonna was cautious enough to keep the incriminating evidence in a safety deposit box in a financial institution controlled by some associates of mine. This evidence is now in my possession."

Poota Bastardo replies, "I cannot thank you enough, Madam President."

"Yes, well, we shall see." After reaching into her desk drawer and opening up a new file Vladimira Pushkin scans through its documents, and continues by saying,

"Your rather unorthodox enterprise has proved to be very profitable indeed, my dear Poota. I believe that you have accrued some forty billion dollars. About half is deposited or managed by institutions controlled by some of my very dear friends."

Poota Bastardo's already puffy slit-like eyes narrow even further. She regards Vladimira Pushkin with growing suspicion and asks, "Are you expecting *me* to repay my country's debts from my own personal assets?"

Vladimira Pushkin stands up and moves to the other side of her desk. After sitting down on one corner and facing the Argentinian she replies reassuringly, "Of course not."

She crosses her legs. Her skirt rides up ever so slightly, revealing a small amount of thigh just above her knee. Poota Bastardo glances down briefly at the Russian president's perfect milky white skin. Vladimira Pushkin draws her riding crop over the leathery skin of her guest's cheek. A shiver of almost electric intensity courses through Poota Bastardo's body. She is unsure as to whether it is sensual in nature or one of pure terror.

"Wh-wh-what do you want?" stutters Poota Bastardo.

Vladimira Pushkin smiles before replying,

"*You* ... are going to help me create history."

****

A large group of journalists and several television crews are gathered to witness the truly historic event of a British deputy prime minister's release from incarceration. Nick Lafarge steps out of the police station where he has spent the night. He is still wearing the same torn clothing, he has a thick lip, and the bruise around his right eye has turned blue-black.

"Bloody rozzers," he mutters under his breath.

He lights a cigarette and makes his way through the police cordon that protects him from the crowd. He ignores the journalists' questions and gets into his ministerial car.

"Right, off to Number 10," he says brusquely.

His driver wrinkles his nose and looks into the rear-view mirror.

"Perhaps, sir, you would prefer to bathe and change your clothes before meeting the prime minister?"

"No, I bloody well wouldn't. Just shut up and get a move on," shouts Nick Lafarge. He is more than a little angry.

A few minutes later his car pulls up outside Number 10. Lafarge gets out and enters the building. He is met by Sir Percy Talleewacker, the Cabinet Secretary.

"Well, that was rather a scrape. The police tell me that Boner accused you of throwing the first punch," he says.

"The bloody liar. He's in for a proper hiding next time I see him."

"I would advise against that. The PM is already so angry that he could crack Brazil nuts between his cheeks, and I don't mean the ones either side of his mouth," replies Sir Percy.

"*He's* angry. Bloody nerve. Where is he?"

"He's waiting for you in the Cabinet Room," replies Sir Percy.

They both make their way to the Cabinet Room.

Berkeley Hunt is reading through some official documents. Without knocking Nick Lafarge bursts into the room, with Sir Percy Talleewacker close on his heels.

"What the bloody hell do you mean, having me banged up all night! And how the hell did you manage it?" shouts Lafarge.

"Thank you, Sir Percy. Please excuse us," says Berkeley Hunt quite calmly. Sir Percy leaves the room and closes the door. Lafarge paces the room angrily.

"Punishment," continues Berkeley Hunt.

"Punishment? For what?" shouts Nick Lafarge.

"For embarrassing Her Majesty's Government ... and me."

"Well, that's a joke. I doubt there's a person on the planet who could embarrass you. You've spent a lifetime perfecting the art of embarrassing yourself. And how did you get the plod to keep me there?"

"I had Sir Percy tell them that it was a matter of national security and that your life was in danger. Anyway, do you know who I had screaming down the phone at me for half an hour yesterday?" replies Berkeley Hunt.

"Let me guess. Mrs Endlessly Insipid herself," replies Lafarge, taking a seat.

"Yes, Hilary bloody Poinswatter. Deputy prime ministers of Her Majesty's Government do not start punch-ups with members of the public, especially involving the US vice president."

"You're forgetting what that Welshman did."

"Forget the Welshman! After that senator croaking on board one of our submarines we've now got this. That bloody woman loathes us more than ever," shouts Berkeley Hunt.

"You mean she loathes *you* more than ever. After all, no one is going to forget in a hurry what you did to her at Buckingham Palace last year," replies Nick Lafarge, drily.

"You know damn well that was an accident, so drop it!"

"Women tend not to forget things like that, especially a spiteful old sow like Poinswatter," replies Lafarge, scratching his chin.

"Stop changing the subject, Nick. I could ask you to resign for conduct unbecoming of a minister of the Crown."

"Ha. Fat chance."

"In which case I may just have to sack you."

"Go ahead," replies Lafarge, nonchalantly. "Because my party won't follow you without me as deputy PM. You'll be in a minority government. And since you couldn't organise an orgy in a knocking shop – let alone run a government – there'll have to be a general election, which you know you'll lose."

Berkeley Hunt pauses for a few seconds, as though he is in deep contemplation, and then replies,

"You're quite right. I'm not going to ask you to resign, nor am I going to sack you."

Nick Lafarge has always felt he has had the upper hand against Berkeley Hunt. He is thus surprised by Hunt's casual response.

"What are you up to?" he asks suspiciously.

In a most amiable manner Berkeley Hunt replies, "I'd like you to do something for me."

Lafarge asks, after injecting a large amount of scepticism, "Really? And what might that be?"

"I would be very grateful if you would drop your support for the tax reform bill," replies Berkeley Hunt.

Nick Lafarge bursts out laughing.

"You're on a roll today, Hunt. First you suggest that I resign. And then you want me to abandon a cornerstone principle of my party policy that's supported by members of your *own* party ... Not a chance in hell."

Lafarge laughs some more.

"Oh, yes, and I forgot about that Scottish harpy, Turbot. There's no way she'll abandon tax reform." Lafarge continues to laugh.

Unusually, Berkeley Hunt stares impassively at Nick Lafarge, who becomes mildly unnerved at Hunt's uncharacteristically cool demeanour.

"We'll get to Patricia in a minute, but first let's talk about you," says Berkeley Hunt as he passes a file to Nick Lafarge.

Lafarge takes the file and begins to read through its numerous documents.

"Very interesting. Where did you get this?" asks Lafarge.

"Does it matter?"

"No, but I can guess."

"What is it, Nick? Five million quid in unpaid back tax? Very well hidden, that money of yours. All that unpaid tax deliberately secreted away ... that's a *very* long prison sentence. I always wondered why you were so keen on the tax reform bill. The amnesty and immunity clause, requiring only one year's return and declaration ... That would have saved your bacon at a bargain-basement price."

"This is all very interesting, Hunt, but it's not going to help your cause."

"Really? If all this were to be made public *now* ... I'm not sure who would string you up first. Your party, the tax office, or your wife?" replies Berkeley Hunt.

"That's not what I meant, all this," he says, waving the file in the air. "Might get me in the slammer, but there's still Turbot. Even without me and my party she has enough votes to get the bill through."

Berkeley Hunt slides over another file to Nick Lafarge's side of the table.

"This will persuade Patricia, I think. I suggest you go and have a talk with her."

The deputy prime minister is silent for a few moments as he stares at the file in front of him. And then he looks up and replies, "You know, Hunt, this isn't your style – blackmail, that is – particularly as it's Turbot you're also putting the squeeze on. And *I know* that you've got a thing for her."

Berkeley Hunt goes slightly red in the face.

"Don't be ridiculous. There's nothing going on between us."

"Oh I know *that*," replies Nick Lafarge. He is a sanguine individual – a cool customer, one might say. He knows he's been rumbled and that his options are non-existent. Nevertheless he refuses to be intimidated by his circumstances, and also wants to let Berkeley Hunt know that he too is on the ball.

"It's just that I wonder what sort of fantasies about Turbot are running wild in your head as that little bint in Bayswater is thrashing your buttocks black and blue."

58

Berkeley Hunt goes an even darker shade of red.

"Look, do we have a deal or not?"

"Of course, but I want all the documents, copies, and originals when I've secured her end of the arrangement. Agreed?"

"Certainly," replies Berkeley Hunt.

Nick Lafarge stands up, picks up the files, and makes his way to the door. Then he stops and turns around to face Berkeley Hunt.

"You know, Hunt, three months ago you were all in favour of tax reform. Now ... well, you're not. What is it that your gobshite of a brother has got on you that has scared you fartless?"

"I don't know what you mean," replies Berkeley Hunt, and wrinkles his nose. "Oh yes ... probably best if you had a shower and changed your clothes before you see Patricia. You smell worse than a yak that's fallen into a cesspit. Goodbye, Nick."

Berkeley Hunt goes back to reading through his documents.

A few minutes later his mobile rings. He answers it.

"Hello, Humpty ..."

"Bruiser, must you really—?"

"Calm down. Have you seen Lafarge?"

"He left a few minutes ago. I think he's off to see Patricia, but unless he has a shower she's likely to kick him out."

"Knew we could count on him. Rather like him, really," replies Mike Hunt.

"Well, you have a funny way of showing it. I doubt he's that thrilled at being blackmailed."

"He'll take it in his stride. He knows it's all part of the game. He's almost one of us – no breeding, of course, but his heart's in the right place."

"What do you mean, 'His heart's in the right place'? That man has no conscience."

"Exactly. As Father used to say, 'Life's too short for a conscience. You can't get ahead if you've got one.' But then you never paid much attention to Father's more meaningful aphorisms."

"Well, I hope this all doesn't end up going down the Swanee," replies Berkeley Hunt wearily.

"Why should it? When the bill is dropped nothing's going to change."

Berkeley Hunt replies with a little more courage than usual.

"Well, I hope so, Bruiser, because that's what you said when you and Lafarge twisted Dave's arm into offering the voters a referendum on the European Community. As the whole world is now fully aware, the outcome has caused a complete bugger's muddle. Neither man, God, nor beast can sort it out."

"You're overreacting, Humpty. This is totally different, and look on the bright side. It's you who's getting the blame for the outcome of the referendum."

"Exactly. *I'm* getting the blame ... Hold on, how is that the bright side? I had nothing to do with the bloody referendum. I didn't even vote."

"Precisely. If someone who ordinarily was regarded as intelligent and competent were to take the blame it would cause an even greater crisis of confidence in the government, and dent the national psyche."

"What do you mean?"

"It's much handier to blame the buffoon in times of crisis. It makes people feel better about themselves and their own shortcomings. So in a way you have performed an outstanding service, and are really something of a national hero. Facing the full force of scorn and derision from the whole world has proved a remarkably good distraction from the incompetence of HM Government as a whole."

"Well ... I ... I hadn't ... quite thought of it that way," replies Berkeley Hunt, in confused contemplation. And then, after a few seconds, as soon as he suspects that his brother might be teasing him, he raises his voice and says, "You're winding me up."

"Not a bit," replies Mike Hunt innocently, while suppressing a laugh.

Now a little more annoyed at having been ridiculed, Berkeley Hunt raises his voice.

"Well, Bruiser, you can make fun of me, but what happened to Dave wasn't funny at all. Look at what the referendum result did for his state of mind, the poor sod. He still hasn't recovered from his nervous breakdown. He had to resign from the only job he ever wanted."

"Yes, being prime minister was the only real job he ever had, if you can call politics a real job. I'm also not surprised that he didn't have the guts to stick it out on the backbenches. He was always a pathetic and snivelling flaky little toad at school, always sucking up to someone. I thought your *friendship* had cooled off after Oxford."

"Not at all. We've always been very close, and I'm concerned about him."

"Good God! After all these years you don't mean to tell me you and he are *still* ... bum chums?" replies Mike Hunt, a little horrified.

"What! Where the hell did you get ever get that idea?"

"Well, you and he were always hanging around together, taking showers at the same time and spending a lot of time together in the bogs, as I recall."

"That's ... that's ... just nonsense," replies Berkeley Hunt, trying to sound composed and unruffled.

Not entirely certain as to the honesty of his brother's reply, Mike Hunt replies, "If you say so, Humpty. Right, enough of the childhood reminiscing. Got to get back to work. Let me know how it goes with Turbot," Mike Hunt says, and hangs up the phone.

****

Vladimira Pushkin stands up from the corner of her desk and paces up and down behind Poota Bastardo. While slapping her riding crop in the palm of her hand she begins.

"Phase One … To avoid suspicion about his departure from this world it will be announced shortly that Primadonna will be remaining behind after your visit, to assist in the preparations for next year's football tournament—"

Poota Bastardo interrupts the president and says, "But that will only work for a few days, won't it?"

"Please do not interrupt me again, Poota," replies Vladimira Pushkin with a smile, but her tone is unmistakably rebuking.

"In two days he will have left on a private plane back to Buenos Aires. The plane will have crashed in the Atlantic. His body will be discovered by a passing Russian freighter. Three days later you will announce that Primadonna was the head of a global narcotics network and that a number of your Cabinet ministers and members of Parliament were also involved in this conspiracy."

"I can't possibly do that. All those people are innocent. No one will believe me," cries the Argentine president.

Vladimira Pushkin throws her head back and laughs at the irony. And, while slapping the riding crop even harder into her palm, she says, "Indeed, my dear Poota. All are innocent, and considerably less tarnished than yourself. The guilty protecting the innocent … Quite a novel concept, don't you agree?" she says, continuing to laugh.

"I don't really see the humour, Madam President, as I would be likely to be impeached for making such groundless accusations," replies Poota Bastardo, a touch petulantly.

Vladimira Pushkin goes back to her chair and sits down.

"I am surprised that you have survived as long as you have, both as president and as a peddler of narcotics. Naturally, over the last several months, my security and intelligence services have been manufacturing the requisite evidence against these individuals."

She hands over a list.

Poota Bastardo looks through the list and replies, "These people all have unblemished reputations and are considered to be completely incorruptible—"

"Which is why it will appear all the more credible," says Vladimira Pushkin as she interrupts Poota. "After all, no one is going to believe that you contrived such compelling evidence against such upstanding and righteous individuals. Call it reverse psychology if you will."

"I'm not so sure. I really don't think—"

She is interrupted once more.

"Phase Two ... Two days after these individuals have been arrested you will announce that they were also involved in a plot to overthrow your government ... Yes, yes, before you ask, that evidence has also been manufactured. You will declare martial law and dissolve your parliament on the pretext of a possible impending coup."

"This is madness," replies Poota Bastardo, raising her voice in an almost pleading tone. "Even if you ... I mean, even if I can convince the people of these crimes and this conspiracy they will regard the imposition of martial law as an opportunistic attempt to revert to a dictatorship. It will never work. There'll be riots."

"Phase One is a calculated risk. We estimate the probability of success to be at 90 per cent. You are of course correct, my dear Poota. For Phase Two the pill will need to be sweetened. Therefore you will announce that considerable tax cuts, welfare payments, and similar rebates will be returned to the people—"

"What? The country's nearly bankrupt. I can't find one single peso to buy toilet paper for the presidential palace, let alone finance wholesale tax cuts."

"Which is why, dear Poota, the money will be reimbursed from your accounts held with my friends."

Poota Bastardo almost chokes on her brandy and, in a rasping voice, says, "M-m-my money ..."

"A small price to pay, I'm sure you'll agree, for your liberty. And, in any event, you are here to help create history. The rewards for so doing are considerable."

"What do you hope to gain out of this?" asks Poota Bastardo, considerably puzzled and not a little anxious.

"That is of no matter for the present. You are simply to follow your instructions," replies Vladimira Pushkin.

While doing her best to conceal her obvious apprehension, and countering as defiantly as she can, Poota says, "What if I refuse? It is not as though you can eliminate me as well. There will be too many questions and a great deal of suspicion. The international community will become even more wary of you than is already the case."

"Did you really think I would not anticipate such a response? Very well … I am sure that Interpol would be most gratified to receive Primadonna's evidence concerning your illicit activities, and I would be more than delighted to escort you personally to Interpol headquarters."

Poota Bastardo's tanned leathery skin loses some of its colour.

Pushkin continues.

"Not only would they be delighted, I'm sure, to see you in prison for many, many years, but nearly every penny you possess would be sequestrated, and Primadonna's death could be quite easily explained in those circumstances.

"But enough of this nonsense," she concludes, the disdain evident in her voice.

"It appears that I have very few choices," says Poota Bastardo, gloomily.

"You have no choices, dear Poota. Do not think that once you return to Buenos Aires that you can escape this arrangement. Your personal bodyguard has been replaced with men loyal to me, and I have ensured the complete cooperation of your military. You should consider also that if the truth behind who is the *real* head of the narcotics network were to be revealed to your countrymen that you would have *nowhere* to run. Your circumstances would, in all probability, become *terminal*."

Knowing that she is trapped, but equally that Vladimira Pushkin needs her cooperation, Poota Bastardo replies with a grim sardonic smile and says, "Very well."

"Good," says Vladimira. She presses a button on her desk and two guards enter the room.

"I think that is all. Goodbye, dear Poota. We will be in touch."

Poota Bastardo stands up and shuffles her bulky frame towards the door. She leaves the room, escorted by Kronsteen.

Kronsteen walks back and stands waiting by the side of the desk. Vladimira Pushkin stands up and, while turning towards him, says casually, "Get someone to clean up that mess in the courtyard." Kronsteen is silent. She looks up into his cold, hard face.

"Later," he growls.

She raises her riding crop and strikes him across the cheek. A cruel smile begins to form on his face as he wipes away the trickle of blood. He moves forward and grips the Russian president's hair behind her neck and smears his blood across her mouth. Her lips part, her bosoms heave, and she becomes breathless.

As their mouths lock she bites down hard on his lower lip. He pushes her back on to the desk and, clutching the top of her blouse, he roughly rips it off. She reaches up, grabs his head, and pulls his mouth towards hers once more.

Day Eight

Nick Lafarge is shown into Patricia Turbot's Westminster office. She is expecting him. Like nearly everyone else in politics, she detests him. And she detests him more than most, as she cannot abide his boorish, misogynistic manner. She keeps him waiting for a few moments. And then, without looking up, she abruptly asks,

"Well, what do want?"

"I'm withdrawing my support for the tax reform bill," he says.

She looks up at him and begins to laugh.

"That looks more painful in person than it does on the TV."

She continues to laugh.

Nick Lafarge touches his swollen, bruised eye and replies with some scorn, "You won't be laughing in a minute, love."

"Really? Why? What are you going to do, headbutt me? Go on, I dare you," she replies, and laughs some more.

"Now, there's a thought, and I've certainly had worse ideas," he says drily, as he sits down.

"I'm sure you think so, but none quite as bad as withdrawing your support for the bill. Your party will crucify you, particularly as everyone knows I don't need your support to get it through. So, needless to say, you don't have my support for your immigration bill."

"I actually came here to be nice to you, Pat."

"Go on. This should be good."

"As I'm a gentleman I'm going to ask you politely to drop the tax reform bill."

Patricia Turbot laughing yet again replies, "You ... a gentlemen... ha! There are sex offenders in prison who have more respect for women than you."

"That wasn't very nice. And here I am, trying to do you a good turn. Tell me, why are you supporting the bill?" he asks, trying to disturb her composure. "It'll hit Reggie really hard."

Unbeknownst to Nick Lafarge, Patricia Turbot's husband Reggie is a serial tax evader, like he is. And so the amnesty and immunity clause in the bill is of significant economic benefit to both Turbot and her husband.

"My husband's tax affairs are none of your business," she replies angrily. "And besides, you know perfectly well that it will benefit the hard-pressed people of Scotland, including the inbred cretins who voted for you."

"That's very funny indeed. We'll come back to your love of the great unwashed in a moment." Nick Lafarge places the laptop he has been carrying on Patricia Turbot's desk, opens it up, and turns it around to face her.

"Now I *did* say I was going to be nice and polite. Well, now I'm not." He presses a key on the laptop and a recording begins to play.

Patricia Turbot stares impassively at herself on the screen. She is writhing around naked on her bed with Malcolm, her aide. On the screen she is saying in a lascivious tone,

"Ooh, Malcolm, you *are* a bad boy. Where did you learn to do that? Never mind. Just do it again, only ... more slowly this time."

Nick Lafarge presses the stop button.

"I must say, Pat, I was entertained for hours by your most enthusiastic display. You're wasted in politics. Think of all those men you could be doing a *really* worthwhile service for in front of the camera."

Patricia Turbot stares coldly at Lafarge and remains remarkably unperturbed.

"You're behind the times, Nick," she says. "If this is some sort of threat, or an attempt at blackmail, you've fallen woefully short. No one cares who's jumping in and out of bed with who any longer."

"I know that. I just wanted *you* … to know that I'd seen you in the buff in all your glory," he replies, and laughs.

"Really? Well, you can look forward to a nice retirement in a dosshouse somewhere when Reggie's done with you."

Patricia Turbot is now shouting. She continues, "This is an outrageous invasion of my privacy!"

"Calm down, love. This has got nothing to do with me. This is Mike Hunt's handiwork."

"Berkeley's brother? You and he are thick as thieves, so it has everything to do with you. Where did you get it?"

"It's not me this time. As to where it—"

"Does Berkeley Hunt know?" she interrupts.

Nick Lafarge is silent for a split second. The last thing that he wants is for Patricia Turbot to confront Berkeley Hunt, and thus the possibility of exposing his own misconduct. He lies.

"No. He hasn't a clue. As to where it came from … if you watch some more I'm sure you'll work it out."

He presses a key to restart the recording. The heated exchange between Patricia Turbot and Malcolm a few days earlier is shown.

Patricia Turbot:

Grow up, Malcolm. Money matters a very great deal. Do you really think I want to give up our houses in Marbella and Barbados to go and live with you on a housing estate in Glasgow?

Nick Lafarge plays another extract.

Patricia Turbot:

Oh, be serious. You don't really want to turn Scotland into a workers' paradise, do you? As for independence, that's to be avoided at all costs.

Yet another extract is played.

Patricia Turbot:

The people ... ha! People will believe anything if you come up with a convincing enough narrative. And no one is more susceptible to a good yarn than a Scotsman with an inferiority complex and more testosterone than brain cells ...

"That'll do, I think," says Lafarge, closing up his laptop . "Very foolish of you to keep recording after you'd finished with the bedroom gymnastics, don't you think? So, you see, this is no invasion of your privacy. It's your own handiwork!"

Patricia Turbot begins to lose some of her composure and replies, "I can see why Hunt wants to scotch the bill, but why do you? What's he got on you?"

"Nothing," he lies. "And I'm not here to talk about me. I'm here to give you some good advice."

He stands up and lights a cigarette. Patricia Turbot eyes him coldly and contemptuously as he paces around the room. He continues by saying, "Now I'll agree that your bedroom acrobatics will only raise a titter or two on the Internet. Then there's your and Reggie's voyeuristic interests. That'll get a few more laughs. And of course there's your money-grubbing, grasping tendencies. Well, that'll turn a lot of people off, particularly the Trots and the Marxists in the SIP. I'm also sure that dear old Reggie won't be best pleased at the whole world discovering that 'wee Jimmy' can't stand to attention.

"But far more important than any of that is that your supporters will discover you have been conning them for years with promises of independence and prosperity. Oh, yes, and what you *really* think of them.

"These are unforgivable sins. Now, putting all this together, I think I can say with some confidence that your precious Sweaties will burn you as a witch. The Dolphin Square scandal would look like shoplifting in comparison. So do yourself a favour, eh, Pat?"

Nick Lafarge gives her a hard, ruthless stare.

Patricia Turbot remains silent, but gives him an icy glare in return.

****

Berkeley Hunt is seated at his desk in his office at Number 10. He is slowly nodding off to sleep. He begins to dream.

In his dream both of his hands are handcuffed to Penny's bed, and he is in his bondage leathers. Patricia Turbot, who is fully clothed in a business suit, places a blindfold across his face and says, "No peeking, now, while I change."

Berkeley Hunt licks his lips as he hears the sounds of Patricia Turbot removing her clothes. He senses a woman's hand move towards his face, and his heart beats faster.

"Are you ready for your surprise?" asks Patricia Turbot seductively. The blindfold is removed. In front of him stands Hilary Poinswatter, president of the United States, dressed as a dominatrix carrying a very nasty, vicious-looking whip. While glaring at him she gives him a particularly ferocious snarl as she cracks the whip.

"Argh!" he screams.

A mobile phone rings. Berkeley Hunt is jolted from his nightmare as he realises that it is in fact his phone that is ringing. Still groggy and yawning, he answers it.

"Err ... Hello?"

"Were you asleep, you lazy sod?" asks Mike Hunt.

"Err ... well ... um ..."

"Never mind. Well, have you seen Lafarge? And what did Turbot say?"

"Patricia has agreed to drop the bill, subject to the review by the independent think tanks," replies Berkeley Hunt.

"Excellent. No more innovative policy programmes, Humpty. It's not why you were put in the job."

"It wasn't my initiative. It was Patricia and Lafarge's," replies a protesting Berkeley Hunt.

"Yes, well you shouldn't have let it get as far as it did. By the way, did you watch the video of Turbot?"

"No ... well, not the intimate bits. I have too much regard for Patricia," replies Berkeley Hunt. He can't work out himself whether the latter part of his reply is the truth, a half-truth, or a downright lie.

"Ha. Tosh and nonsense. Have to say, she's a right little goer. Glad I kept a copy of the disk. It'll provide hours of entertainment when the wife's out in the evening."

"What! You can't do that. Lafarge gave his word."

"Don't worry, Humpty. It'll be kept safely locked away. I won't use it. That would be breaking the rules of the game. After all, I wouldn't want someone to do the same thing to me about something I would rather keep quiet, would I?"

"As a matter of interest, where did you get the disk?" asks Berkeley Hunt.

"Stroke of luck, really. A few days ago a young chap called Malcolm came to see me—"

"Malcolm, Patricia's aide?"

"Yes."

"Wonder why he didn't come to me."

"Asked him the same question. Like everyone else, he thinks you're an idiot and that you have some sort of infatuation with Turbot. At least that's what Turbot said to him, and of—"

"Well ... that's just ... just nonsense," interrupts Berkeley Hunt, trying to sound unflustered.

"Which bit? That you're an idiot, or that you are infatuated with Turbot?"

"Both! ... Well, all right, I'm not that clever, but I'm certainly not infatuated with Patricia," lies Berkeley Hunt, unconvincingly.

"Well, if you say so, but it's just as well that he came to me. We both know that you have no stomach for blackmail. And you

71

wouldn't have thought about getting Lafarge to do the dirty work, let alone been able to compel him to do so, without my help."

"Hold on a mo ... Malcolm's on the disk as well. So why did he hand it over?" asks Berkeley Hunt, more than a little stupidly.

"Honestly, Humpty, I despair of you sometimes. Clearly he had a broken heart and was obviously aggrieved at being personally and politically betrayed. Can you believe it? The young fool actually swallowed all that guff for years about independence in a worker's paradise."

"Well, *I* did too ... until a couple of days ago."

"Yes, well, that's only to be expected. He's a strange young chap. He was shabbily dressed, and didn't want any money for the disk ..."

"What's so strange about that? There *are* some people who have a conscience and principles, Bruiser."

"Perhaps, but he'd obviously been to public school, which is why I thought it strange that he didn't want any money. Idealistic fellow – and dangerous, to boot. Said that he just wanted 'the truth' to come out."

"Well, obviously that's not going to happen now. What's he going to do when he finds out that you've buried the information?" asks Berkeley Hunt.

"What can he do? He doesn't have a copy of the disk. If he starts shouting the odds it'll be his word against Turbot's. I'm glad there aren't other chaps like him. Imagine if there were more people in politics and business who wanted to tell the truth. God's trousers, the world would be in complete pandemonium."

"I meant to ask last time ... How did you find out that Lafarge was a serial tax dodger? From the tax office?" asks Berkeley Hunt.

"Ha! The tax office? The Permanent Secretary at the tax office wouldn't be able to find his trousers even if he was wearing them, let alone a tax dodger. No, Goldstein Brothers keep extensive files on most of the tax dodgers in the country. Comes in very handy from time to time." replies Mike Hunt.

"Are you serious?"

"Oh, yes, and of course the security services have been keeping an eye on Lafarge for years. Ever since he was at that South London public school, in fact, so they too are aware of his numerous misdeeds."

"Ever since he was at school! What the hell could he have been doing at school that would interest the security services?"

"Well, he was a not-so-secret member of a supposedly secret, but actually, not-so-secret neo-Nazi organisation that had been penetrated by our domestic intelligence service."

"How the hell do *you* know all of this and *I* don't?" asks Berkeley Hunt, incredulously.

"How do I know? Well you probably didn't know this, but before you were my fag, Dickie Querelove, the former head of the Joint Intelligence Committee (JIC) was. The reason you don't know any of this is because Lafarge was a minor at the time. So it has no bearing on his security clearance, nor indeed any relevance to party politics, so the security services aren't obliged to tell you."

"Bloody marvellous ... I've got a Nazi in the Cabinet and I'm not allowed to know," replies Berkeley Hunt drily.

"Do you know why he got expelled?"

"I didn't think Querelove got expelled," says a confused Berkeley Hunt.

"Not Querelove, you idiot. Lafarge. Apparently they wouldn't make him a prefect, and in his rage he kicked some little African boy in the third form straight through a window. Not something even I would do. Well, not through a window, anyway. Rumour has it that he also tried to have his wife done in—"

"What?"

"Probably just malicious gossip, so I wouldn't worry about it."

"I've got a Nazi with murderous inclinations, *in* the Cabinet, second in line to the nuclear codes, and you're telling me not worry about it."

"Relax, Humpty, it's not as though he's going to have you knocked off. He knows, as do I that you're far too important."

"Really? Do you think so?"

"Think what?"

"That I'm too important to be … err … bumped off."

"Humpty, take it from me, you're indispensable. I couldn't run the country without you."

Day Fourteen

"Congratulations, my dear Poota."

The polite yet undeniably cold and assured voice of Vladimira Pushkin startles Poota Bastardo somewhat. Although the Argentine president has been expecting her telephone call she is nonetheless unnerved by her counterpart's composure.

"Congratulations ... How can you say that? Fifteen people were killed during the protests at the imposition of martial law, and I've had to lock up ten times as many," replies Poota Bastardo. She is clearly fretting.

"You are worrying unnecessarily. When you announce tomorrow that your people will be twenty billion dollars better off the unrest will subside."

"Yes, and *I'll* be twenty billion poorer," replies the Argentine president, who is by now almost on the verge of heart failure.

"Think of it as an investment in your future—"

"My future? That, I have to say, is not looking particularly secure, not with all your men 'guarding' me and several hundred Russian soldiers in the capital," interrupts the Argentine president angrily.

"They are there for your protection, dear Poota, not to cause you harm."

"Well ... if, as you say, the people will be placated by my generosity, I don't see why I need them around, nor indeed your soldiers," replies Poota Bastardo, a little tersely.

"One can never be too careful. You should be flattered. Your safety is of paramount importance to me. When we have completed the final phase of my plan you will be free to resume your previous, and very lucrative, activities."

"I will?" replies Poota Bastardo, more than a little surprised.

"Certainly. And, when my plan comes to fruition, you will be more popular than any leader in your country's history. You will be able to retain absolute power with your people's blessing, and not even you will be able to dream about the amount of money you will make.

"Now to business …

"Phase Three …"

****

Berkeley Hunt is in his office at Number 10, reading through a document. Once again he begins to nod off to sleep, but before he can do so his desk phone rings.

"Humpty?"

Replying somewhat groggily, "Err … yes?"

"You weren't asleep again, were you, you lazy sod?"

"Err, no. I was reading through a briefing note on the state of the health service."

"Well, that's enough to make anyone fall asleep, I suppose. I don't know why you don't privatise the damn thing, but then again I suppose there'd be a hue and cry from the plebs, and open revolt."

"Is there something you wanted, Bruiser?"

"What? Oh, yes, that nuclear power station. You can give the go-ahead to the construction now."

"What?"

"Frimley Point D, you idiot."

"I know where you mean, Bruiser. But six months ago you told me that we needed to undertake a full review of the project because of the security risks of having the Chinese involved, and that you thought the Frogs might go bankrupt long before the project was completed," replies Berkeley Hunt, by now both perplexed and incensed.

"Is that what I said? Oh, never mind about that …"

"What do you mean, 'Never mind'? Hold on a minute … I thought you were in favour of renewables and wind turbines, and that was also another reason for the review. So what's with the sudden change of mind?"

"No change of mind. And of course I'm in favour of wind turbines. I've got twenty of them on my property in Berkshire, and the taxpayer is paying me a small fortune to keep them there."

"I'm going to look a right idiot if I give the go-ahead to the project before the review is completed," replies an anxious Berkeley Hunt.

"Well, no one is going to notice *that*, so I wouldn't worry about it. But do what you like, Humpty. I don't really care whether you give it the go-ahead or not."

"Well why the bloody hell did you get me to instigate the review in the first place?"

"Just returning a favour to an old girlfriend, actually. You remember Daniela, the smouldering little Italian nymph, don't you?"

"Yes, of course, but what has a multi-billion pound project got to do with your old love life?" asks a now exasperated Berkeley Hunt.

"Well, Daniela is the partner at Young & Waterman who's been advising *Nucléaire Électrique de France* on the consultation process for building Frimley Point. I didn't really think she was that clever a girl but she's managed to drag out the whole process for ten years, and she's earned Young & Waterman a very tidy sum from NEF over that time.

"Anyway, she told me she wanted to retire in six months' time and just wanted a short delay so that she could squeeze out a few million more in fees from NEF before she left."

Berkeley Hunt is aghast, but before he can think of a suitable retort there is a knock on his door and Sir Percy Talleewacker enters the room.

Berkeley Hunt lets out a deep sigh.

"Well, Bruiser, got to go. Sir Percy is here, no doubt with some uplifting news," says Berkeley Hunt, with a touch of sarcasm. He hangs up the phone.

"In order to be implemented the Article 66 subsection 6 document on the European Community requires your signature, Prime Minister," says Sir Percy.

Berkeley Hunt blows out his cheeks.

"Oh, God, must I? I don't know why it should be me who has to sign the damn thing. Dave was the one to promise the blasted referendum.

"I mean, for God's sake, I didn't even vote. I was getting thrash— I mean I was at the dentist at the time. As far as I'm concerned it's just going to end up being another stick people will use to beat me over the head with," replies a morose-sounding Berkeley Hunt.

"I'm afraid you must, Prime Minister. Parliament requires it," replies Sir Percy.

"Can't we get Dave to sign it? After all, he was the fool to offer the referendum in the first place."

"I'm afraid not, Prime Minister. He's no longer prime minister. You are. Even if we could there is, as I'm sure you're aware, some dispute as to his err … current status and … err … competency."

Berkeley Hunt blows out his cheeks again and replies, "Oh, very well." He then signs the document.

As he puts his pen down his desk phone rings. He answers it and hangs up after a few seconds. He reaches for his remote control and turns on his TV.

"Who was that?" asks Sir Percy.

"The chief press officer. He said there's something I need to see."

On the TV a news bulletin reports that Poota Bastardo, president of the Argentine nation, has declared martial law and dissolved the Argentine parliament.

"We should probably have seen this coming after that woman had those Cabinet ministers arrested," says Sir Percy, thoughtfully.

"What does all of this have to do with us?" asks Berkeley Hunt.

"The Russians are now more deeply entrenched on the southern flank of the North Atlantic Treaty Alliance (NATA)," replies Sir Percy.

"But they are not allied to Argentina, Sir Percy, are they?"

"Not formally, no. Vladimira Pushkin is far too clever for that. But engineering a coup is just the sort thing she's capable of."

"Are you saying you think all of this has something to do Russia?" As usual Berkeley Hunt is slow on the uptake.

Sounding a little uneasy, Sir Percy replies, "Yes, I do. I suggest we keep a close eye on what's going on."

"By holding a COMA (Cabinet Office Military Assessment) meeting?" asks Berkeley Hunt.

"These things have a habit of being reported in the media and I don't think we want to be tipping our hand to Pushkin just yet, Prime Minister. I'll have a discreet word with the director of the JIC and the Chief of the Defence Staff."

****

Vladimira Pushkin has just ended her telephone call with the Argentine president when there is a knock on her door. Kronsteen opens the door and stands behind the army general while he escorts him to Vladimira Pushkin's desk. Then he moves away and places himself behind his mistress.

The Russian president remains seated, and continues to read through the file she has been studying. The general remains standing to attention, as he has not been asked to sit. She looks up and stretches out her hand. The general passes over the file he has been carrying, and Vladimira Pushkin begins to study its contents.

As the general stands patiently while waiting for the president to speak his gaze wanders about the room. It finally settles on Kronsteen. He notices that the big man has a cut on his cheek and a series of faded scratches on the side of his face, as well as a small bruise on his lip and what appears to be a bite mark on his neck. Being fully aware of Kronsteen's reputation, he is more than a little bewildered as to who could have inflicted such injuries on him within the Kremlin itself.

Vladimira Pushkin looks up, and the general quickly returns his gaze to the Russian president.

"Very good, General. I see that Operation Grand Slam is now ready to be executed. How long before our naval flotilla will be in position?" asks Vladimira Pushkin.

"Six days, Madam President," replies the general.

"Good."

"May I speak freely, Madam President?"

Vladimira Pushkin has never been challenged or queried on anything. However rather than taking offence, she is intrigued by the general's audacity, and replies, "By all means, General."

"I am a little concerned as to how the North Atlantic Treaty Powers will respond to Operation Grand Slam."

"I do not share your concerns, General. There will be no response and no reaction, save for words."

"With respect, Strumpet is no longer in the office of president of the United States. I very much doubt that President Poinswatter will agree to the same sort of secret protocol and treaty that *he* did, which allowed us to annex the Baltic States. President Poinswatter is disposed to being much more belligerent and, unlike President Strumpet is no admirer of yours, nor of Russia's," replies the general, as he mops the sweat from his brow with a handkerchief. He is surprised at the extent of his own courage.

80

Vladimira Pushkin smiles a sardonic smile and replies, "I am pleased that our military academies are producing soldiers who can think, for a change. It's a pity that many of my predecessors chose to have our senior military commanders shot or sent to Siberia.

"Hilary Poinswatter will do nothing. She has other concerns. As you well know, General, the American pivot eastwards has shifted the majority of their resources. Indeed, the current state of affairs in the Middle East is not to their liking either. The North Koreans will add to the distraction, as Grand Slam is about to proceed. And of course my European agents will assist in its successful execution."

Although he knows he is riding his luck the general replies, "Can we be certain about your agents, Madam President? Our British agent is motivated purely for mercenary reasons."

The Russian president fixes the general with a stare as cold as a Russian winter.

"Money is very often the most reliable incentive for betrayal ... but I hope that you are not questioning my judgement, General."

"Err ... no, Madam President. It's ... just ... that I have some concerns. Should Operation Grand Slam not go according to plan, because of the failure of our European agents, our plans for the Middle East may go awry. Our clients in the Middle East are already dismayed by your insistence on a peace process."

"General, as you well know, our deception plan was activated some weeks ago and, according to our intelligence service, it has been accepted by the Western intelligence agencies—"

The general boldly interrupts the president and asks, "Madam President, how can we be certain their acceptance is not a double bluff?"

The Russian president is becoming slightly vexed, so counters, "Yes, yes, yes ... double bluff, triple bluff, quadruple bluff ... It can go on and on, General. Like everything else, strategy and subsequent plans are all calculated risks. *And I* ... never miscalculate.

"The Americans will do nothing. They may even be compelled to be compliant, *precisely* because of the peace process in the Middle East. The British, as you know, *can* do nothing. The French ... well, that drunken old fool Molière spends most of his time in Berlosconti's bordellos and doesn't even care. Now ... if there is nothing else, you may retire, General."

The general mops his brow once more. He puckers up his anus and clinches his cheeks together more tightly. It is all he can do to retain control of his bowels.

"President Bastardo ... Are we certain that she will fulfil her end of the bargain?" he asks.

"She has no choice, General. However, should her part in Operation Grand Slam be successful, it is unlikely but *possible* that not even the release of the files containing her criminal activity will diminish her popularity. She has many good reasons to resent us. As we discussed, please ensure that she is eliminated as soon as Grand Slam is underway, and make arrangements to have her replaced with the gentlemen we have previously selected."

"Very good, Madam President," replies the general as he once again mops his brow with his now sodden handkerchief. He salutes and leaves the room.

Day Eighteen

It is mid morning at Number 10 Downing Street, and a Cabinet meeting has just ended. Berkeley Hunt has chosen to remain behind and work in the Cabinet Room. Nick Lafarge has also chosen to remain, albeit for no other reason than knowing that his presence annoys Berkeley Hunt.

Although it is still morning the deputy prime minister has already made some considerable headway into a bottle of whisky. His feet are on the meeting room table and he is reading his favourite tabloid newspaper, one that has become renowned over many years for its alleged artistic portrayal of the female form.

"What do you think of these hooters?" laughs Nick Lafarge, as he turns the newspaper to face Berkeley Hunt. Berkeley Hunt looks up and shakes his head despairingly.

There is a knock at the door and Sir Percy Talleewacker enters the room.

"Yes, Sir Percy, what can I do for you?" asks Berkeley Hunt.

"The Chief of the Defence Staff, Admiral Turgidly, is here. He wanted a discreet meeting with you, Prime Minister," replies the Cabinet Secretary.

"Well, show him in."

Admiral Turgidly enters the Cabinet Room. He is tall and stands ramrod straight. He has spent most of his career in the Submarine Service. Although he was not to blame, it was while serving as the executive officer on one of Her Majesty's attack submarines in the

83

Falkens War that he accidentally torpedoed the last pod of the North Atlantic whale, thereby causing their extinction.

Berkeley Hunt gestures the admiral to a seat.

"I thought it best, Prime Minister, to present my report to you in person, rather than call for a COMA meeting," begins Admiral Turgidly.

"Well, go on, Admiral," replies Berkeley Hunt patiently.

"Ever since the *coup d'état* in Argentina the Joint Intelligence Committee and the American Central Intelligence Bureau (the CIB) have intensified their reconnaissance and intelligence on Argentine military activity. We've detected an increase in signal traffic from various headquarters and from land and naval units. In fact they've rebased a number of their surface ships and marine units to their base on the River Plate ..."

"They're not still pissed off about the 1930 World Cup final, are they?" quips Nick Lafarge drunkenly.

"Shut up, Nick," interjects Berkeley Hunt. "Why have they done that, Admiral?"

"We're not sure, but if the Russians are behind this then it may be some sort of deception to divert us from Operation Grand Slam, and I suspect that the Argent—"

"Operation Grand Slam ... What's that?" interrupts Nick Lafarge.

"If you bothered to read the intelligence briefings you'd bloody well know," snaps Berkeley Hunt.

"Operation Grand Slam, Deputy Prime Minister, is, we believe, the Russians' plan to annexe Finland," replies the admiral.

"Why would they want to do that? It's a godawful place. It's so bloody cold there that the buggers have to spend most of their time in saunas thrashing each other with branches. Come to think of it, Hunt, it's exactly the sort of place you'd love," replies Nick Lafarge, and bursts out laughing.

Berkeley Hunt goes slightly red and then retorts angrily, "Look, if you haven't got anything constructive to say then I suggest you bugger off. Sorry, Admiral. Please continue."

"As you know, Finland is not a signatory to the North Atlantic Treaty. President Pushkin is therefore probably of the view that the members of NATA are unlikely to respond to Russian aggression against Finland."

"Well, are *we*?" asks a confused Berkeley Hunt.

"Are we what?" asks an equally confused Admiral Turgidly.

"Are we unlikely to respond to Russian aggression against Finland?" replies a slightly exasperated Berkeley Hunt.

"That's a political decision, Prime Minister. You'll have to consult with the heads of government of the Alliance."

"Well, if Strumpet were still president he'd probably twist our arm again to do nothing," interjects Nick Lafarge.

"I know it was before my time, but I must admit that I don't really understand why Strumpet refused to support the defence of the Baltic States," muses Berkeley Hunt aloud.

"Well, that's easy. He's always been partial to totty, particularly Slavic totty – God knows he married enough of 'em. He's had the hots for Pushkin for years – probably 'cos she looks like that bint he married. The one he met in that knocking shop in Bratislava," replies Lafarge.

"I suspect it's a little more complicated than that, Deputy Prime Minister. Fortunately President Strumpet is no longer in office. However, perhaps we had better return to the matter at hand. What do you think our response should be, Admiral?" asks Sir Percy.

"We have been planning for this possibility for some time, of course – and, naturally, have been in close contact with the Finnish military. But if you're asking my opinion, Sir Percy, we can't, on this occasion, allow the Russians into Finland. The Poles, in particular, are becoming nervous."

"Nothing new there. Kaczka has always been twitchy," replies Lafarge, referring to the Polish prime minister.

"As I said, this could be some sort of deception plan," begins Admiral Turgidly. "And it seems to me that they could be making a move on the Falken Islands."

"They got a sound beating the last time they tried that," remarks Nick Lafarge.

"Indeed, Deputy Prime Minister, but that was more than thirty years ago. Their military capability is much more modern and proficient today," replies the admiral.

Berkeley Hunt's phone rings. He picks it up and says, "He's here now? Err … send him up in a couple of minutes," and then hangs up. He turns to Sir Percy and the admiral and continues with what they had just been discussing.

"Right. Well, I'll give that old bat in the White House a call and see what she has to say. If there are any developments please let me know, Admiral. Thank you."

Admiral Turgidly and Sir Percy Talleewacker leave the room.

Two minutes later, and without knocking, Mike Hunt enters the Cabinet Room. Nick Lafarge remains seated and eyes him coolly.

"Would you mind, Lafarge? I'd like to talk to my brother alone," says Mike Hunt, nonchalantly. The deputy prime minister remains motionless for a few seconds, and then very deliberately and slowly stands up and walks towards Mike Hunt. He stops almost toe-to-toe with the banker. Berkeley Hunt observes the two men anxiously. Nick Lafarge glares at Mike Hunt, who returns the glare with a cool, sardonic smile.

"I'll get you next time Hunt," says the deputy prime minister gruffly.

"Well, you can *always* try," replies Mike Hunt, with a supercilious grin forming on his face. Nick Lafarge turns away and leaves the room.

"I thought for a moment he was going to thump you, Bruiser," says Berkeley.

"He's not that daft," replies Mike Hunt, and takes a seat opposite his brother.

"Well, what are you doing here? It's all a bit irregular," asks Berkeley Hunt.

"Just came to drop off Lafarge's tax files. Didn't want to risk losing them in the post or getting them lost by some half-witted delivery boy. Oh yes, bumped into the party chairman, he asked me to drop off these documents for your signature." He hands Berkeley Hunt the folders he has been carrying and asks, "So, anything interesting happening, Humpty?"

"Think the Argies may be up to something."

"Really?" he replies, affecting boredom as he picks up Nick Lafarge's newspaper.

Berkeley Hunt fails to pick up on his brother's affectation of boredom and continues by saying, "Yes. Troop and naval movements, increased military signals traffic ... Something's afoot."

Mike Hunt looks up and folds the newspaper below his eyeline.

"Really? Now, that *is* interesting. What do you think they're up to?"

"Well, Bruiser, the Chief of the Defence Staff thinks they may be after the Falkens again."

"What? Surely not? They got a good beating last time they tried that."

"That's what Lafarge said, but Admiral Turgidly thinks it a distinct possibility," replies Berkeley Hunt.

"To be honest, Humpty, I wouldn't worry about it. The Argies are practically bankrupt. I doubt that they could afford to pay for a day trip, much less an invasion," says his brother.

"Anyway, gotta go. Things to do." Mike Hunt stands up, puts down the newspaper, and without more ado leaves the room.

Several minutes later Mike Hunt is walking down Whitehall. A self-satisfied smile begins to form on his face.

"Well, well, well, the Argies invading the Falkens. So that's what she's up to eh? How interesting," he says to himself. He takes out his cigarette case, opens it, and lights a small cheroot. He stops, removes his phone from his jacket pocket, and autodials a number.

"Johnny—"

He is, however, interrupted by an elderly and clearly sickly vagrant who approaches him unsteadily and holds out his hand saying, "'Scuse me, guv, any chance of a cup o' tea?"

"Hold on a minute, my good man," replies Mike Hunt amiably, and then continues to speak into his phone.

"Yes, Johnny, I'd like to see the breakdown of all our clients' holdings by asset classes ... yes, including futures and options ... All right, I know, it's a pain, but get it done by this evening and there's a large drink in it for you."

Mike Hunt ends the call. He turns to the elderly vagrant.

"What was it you were saying, old boy?" asks Mike Hunt as he spots a cab and hails it down.

"Any chance of a cup o' tea, guv?"

Mike Hunt turns to the old man once more and, on noticing his outstretched arm, takes a last drag of his small cheroot and then calmly stubs it out on the palm of the old man's hand. The vagrant yells in pain and falls to his knees.

"Thanks awfully. Littering is a *such* a terrible crime," says Mike Hunt as he gets into the cab.

Day Twenty

It is late morning at Number 10 Downing Street. A COMA meeting is taking place. Gathered there are all the relevant members of the British Cabinet, the chiefs of staff, and the heads of the foreign and domestic intelligence services.

"Well, what's to be done?" says Berkeley Hunt, trying to sound as authoritative as he can in an attempt to mask his nervousness.

"I say," begins Nick Lafarge, hiccupping drunkenly, as usual, "that we go in and give those gauchos a good kicking before they even try to occupy the islands. They're only a bunch of poofters and wops. The Boy Scouts could probably give 'em a hiding."

"My wife's a wop ... err, I mean Italian—" Berkeley Hunt's reply is interrupted.

"Well you're lucky, mine's a Kraut, and she's a total cow," says Nick Lafarge.

"Let's try and be serious, shall we? We can't just attack a sovereign state without reason," replies Berkeley Hunt.

"Why not? Teflon Tony and President Rush did it in the Middle East and there was *absolutely* no justification for that. And neither of them even got nicked for it. At least we're defending our people and our territory," retorts the deputy prime minister.

"Gentlemen, I don't think we need to be quite so aggressive," interjects Sir Percy Talleewacker, "We could reinforce the islands with paratroopers or marines, bolstered by some heavy equipment.

That should deter them at least for a while. What do you think, Admiral Turgidly?"

"Yes, well, that wouldn't take more than thirty-six hours. We also have a couple of attack submarines in the area. The nearest, HMS *Argo*, is only two days away. As you know, the Russians have announced that they will be conducting naval exercises with the Argentine navy. This may be a ruse, of course, intended to distract us from their intention to invade, so we'll have to be careful about the rules of engagement," replies the admiral.

"Are we certain that the Argies are *actually* going to invade the Falkens, Admiral?" asks Sir Percy.

"Yes, we're certain. All the facts point to it – a build-up of naval and marine units, increased signals traffic – but despite all this we have no absolute evidence."

"How long before they do, in your estimation, Admiral?" asks Nick Lafarge.

"A week to ten days at the most, Deputy Prime Minister, at their current rate of deployment … and taking account of the tides and the moon."

It is only now that the true enormity of the unfolding events begins to dawn on Berkeley Hunt, and their potential for conflict and calamity. He is reluctant to take any decisive action, and so suggests, "Perhaps we should declare an exclusion zone around the islands, should we?"

"That would only alert the Argentinians to the fact that we are aware of their intentions, which could speed up their operations. We may not be able to get reinforcements there in time," replies Admiral Turgidly.

"What do you suggest, Admiral?" asks Berkeley Hunt, trying not to betray his unease.

"As Sir Percy has suggested, we should reinforce the islands with paratroopers. The two battalions in Poland should do it, supported by a few more fighter bombers."

"Well ... err, I'm not so sure, Admiral ... Do we ... err, really want to provoke them ... I ... I mean?" replies Berkeley Hunt. What little courage he has begins to desert him.

"Provoke them? What are gibbering on about, Hunt? The admiral has already said that they're going to invade," exclaims Nick Lafarge.

"Yes ... well, but there's no proof that's what they're going to do, is there?"

"Prime Minister, if we don't reinforce the islands – and they are captured – we are going to have to assemble a task force to recapture them. That means withdrawing *all* our paratroopers and land units from Poland and elsewhere, about half of our marines, and other significant troop withdrawals from Norway. What with this Grand Slam business we could be leaving both Finland *and* Norway considerably exposed.

"Also, Prime Minister, we would have to deploy the *entire* fleet to retake the islands, which means that the Baltic and the North Sea would be almost defenceless. As our aircraft carriers are still without aircraft we're going to have to beg the French for one of theirs. Otherwise it would be a near impossible task," says the admiral.

"Then there's Kaczka, the Polish prime minister. You know how nervous he is about Pushkin. He wouldn't be happy at degrading his defences, and I doubt that the Americans would be pleased at denuding Western defences in general," says Sir Percy.

"Particularly as that Poinswatter woman loathes you, Hunt. As for Kaczka, he's more paranoid than an entire psychiatric hospital. I wonder what his latest delusion is," says Nick Lafarge.

"I still think he's banging on about those photos of Donald Strumpet in that Moscow hotel room ..." replies Berkeley Hunt, in an attempt to steer the discussion away from the current crisis.

Sir Percy interrupts the deviating and wholly irrelevant musings of the prime minister and his deputy. "I'm sure that it has occurred to everyone that the timing of all of this Argentine and Russian activity is all a bit too coincidental. As Admiral Turgidly pointed out in his report, this may be some sort of deception plan designed to draw away our forces from the defence of Poland and, more importantly, to counter any threat to Finland."

"Well, it's between the Devil and the deep blue sea, then, isn't it? I mean, either way we're going to have to withdraw troops. Tell you what, Hunt, why don't you speak to that old Boche swamp beast and get her to take up the slack with German troops in Poland and Norway. God knows why, but she quite likes you, and the Krauts haven't exactly been pulling their weight recently when it comes to NATA."

"That sounds like a sensible suggestion, Deputy Prime Minister. I suggest, Prime Minister, that you contact the Chancellor of Germany as soon as possible. However, the time is fast approaching when a decision needs to be made in dealing with the threat at hand," says Admiral Turgidly.

Berkeley Hunt puckers up his anus as it begins to twitch feverishly and uncontrollably.

"Err ... I think ... perhaps we should just ... hold off ... for a bit," he stutters.

"What? Hunt, now is not the time to stick your thumb up your rear end," exclaims Nick Lafarge, scornfully.

"Look, I don't want to be dragging us into a war if it can be avoided."

"We're the ones being dragged in, you idiot," exclaims the deputy prime minister.

"Prime Minister, would you at least allow me to send in the submarines?" asks an anxious Admiral Turgidly. "As risky as that may be, it gives us some options – particularly if the Argentinians move more quickly than expected."

Berkeley Hunt's anal twitching jumps into overdrive.

"Err ... well, all right. But I don't want them doing anything that could ... err ... inflame the situation."

"For God's sake, Hunt. Grow a pair," shouts the deputy prime minister.

"I'm the one for the high jump if this all goes pear-shaped, not you, Nick. So button your lip," Berkeley Hunt shouts in reply.

"And reinforcing the islands, Prime Minister?" queries Sir Percy, who is also becoming mildly alarmed at Berkeley Hunt's equivocation.

"Err ... well, I'll ... I'll make a decision in a few days," he replies unsurely.

Sensing that he has support from the Cabinet Secretary, Admiral Turgidly presses the issue.

"Prime Minister, could I move our paratroopers from Poland to St Helen's in the South Atlantic? It would save time if we need to reinforce the Falkens in a hurry."

"Well ... all right, then," replies Berkeley Hunt unsurely, and feeling distinctly uneasy. "But don't do anything with 'em until I've had a couple of days to think about it."

****

Smedley Butler is in his quarters on board HMS *Argo* and is in something of a panic. He has lost his anti-anxiety pills, which keep him from feeling claustrophobic. He frantically searches around for them, upturning his bunk and almost everything else in his quarters that isn't nailed down.

There is a knock at his door. Butler ignores it and continues his search. There is another knock and then he hears the captain's voice.

"Butler, are you there?" Trying to conceal the alarm in his voice the American replies, "Err ... yes, sir. Come in."

The captain enters.

"Are you all right, Butler?" asks the captain, surveying the room. "Bit of a mess in here. Have you lost something?"

"Err, my Bible," lies Smedley Butler.

"Didn't know you were religious?"

"Well, err, I'm not, sir, but it was a gift from my grandmother."

"I see. Well, anyway, we've had a priority action message from CinC Fleet. I'm afraid it's Plan R."

"Plan R, sir?"

"Ah, yes, I forgot that you wouldn't be aware of Plan R. Plan R is a 'possible engagement with hostile forces in a non-NATA capacity', which means, I'm sorry to say, that I'll have to relieve you of your duty, as you are technically a neutral, Butler. We can't have you involved in any sort of contretemps with the Argies. I'm sorry about that, particularly as you've made a remarkably swift recovery from your err ... recent injury."

"I quite understand, sir. I'm just sorry I won't be there with my finger on the trigger if it comes to a shooting war," replies the American.

"Quite. Anyway, don't worry. You're not confined to quarters," says the captain. As he is about to leave he turns back to Butler and continues thoughtfully.

"Fate is a strange thing, don't you think?"

"Sir?"

"Well, a couple of weeks ago we could've put you ashore, what with your injury, and could probably have managed without you. Now we may be going into action, and in all likelihood are going to be undermanned and could probably use you. Only we can't."

"Indeed. Not just fate, but irony as well." This is a particularly insightful reply from Smedley Butler, given that the captain and the majority of the British believe that Americans couldn't distinguish irony from an iguana's armpit. The real irony, of course, is that Americans *do* get irony, only the British don't realise that they do.

Certainly neither man is aware of just how truly ironic events will prove to be.

The captain turns to leave Butler's quarters and notices a heavy leather-bound book on the unit beside Butler's bunk. He picks it up, and after turning back to face Butler once more, enquires, "Is this what you're looking for Butler?"

"Err, yes, sir," lies the commander once more.

The captain laughs and says, "Well, it's just as well you've been relieved. Your eyesight's not up to much. And there was I, thinking that your tackle might be defective."

The captain laughs jovially and Smedley Butler forces himself to do the same, after which the captain leaves. The American returns to hunting for his lost medication.

Day Twenty-Two

It is early morning in Washington DC, and Hilary Poinswatter is in the Oval Office with her personal assistant. Her intercom buzzes, and a secretary announces the arrival of the National Security Advisor.

The National Security Advisor enters the Oval Office just as the president's personal assistant is making her way out. As she leaves she says amiably, "It's good to see you again, Mr Head."

"Likewise, my dear," he replies. The president's personal assistant smiles and leaves the room.

"Take a seat, Dick," says Hilary Poinswatter gesturing the National Security Advisor to seat on the sofa. She moves to join him in an armchair opposite. "That's a fine-looking beaver you have there, Madam President."

"Sorry?" replies the president, suspiciously, as she draws her knees together and pulls down the hem of her skirt.

"Err ... the stuffed beaver on your desk – a very fine specimen, Madam President," he replies.

"Oh ... I see," says Hilary Poinswatter, sounding relieved. "It belongs to Jimmy."

"I didn't know he collected beavers," he mentions quizzically.

"Really? I thought everyone knew," she replies both drily and wearily. "Anyway, to business. What are the North Koreans up to?"

A former deputy director of the Central Intelligence Bureau, the bespectacled Richard Head has not long been the National Security Advisor. He was appointed a little hastily after the death of his predecessor, whose reasons for suicide he has only recently discovered.

Having never had any direct or indirect involvement in extraordinary rendition and torture, illicit assassination attempts, destabilising sovereign states, fermenting or instigating civil conflicts, or starting illegal wars, Richard Head has long been regarded with considerable contempt and suspicion by his former colleagues at the Central Intelligence Bureau. Failing to live up to the bureau's reputation as a world-class global shit-stirrer is a matter of some annoyance and embarrassment to him.

To redeem himself the National Security Advisor is resolved to bring about the overthrow of at least one democratically elected government somewhere in the world.

"North Koreans? Nothing, in my view, Madam President. Simply flexing their muscles, and it's just pretentious posturing. Their fleet entering the South Atlantic is of no consequence and, as you know, the situation is being monitored by our satellites and a carrier battle group."

"I'm more concerned about their missile submarines roaming about the Pacific and the Atlantic, Dick."

"All four are at sea. They can't keep that up for long. Besides, they make so much noise I'm surprised they can't be heard in Kansas," he replies caustically. "So they don't pose any credible threat. It's just a show of strength on their part," he concludes.

"Well, perhaps we should leave our discussion about North Korean military capabilities for our joint meeting with the chiefs of staff."

"As you wish, Madam President."

"Now, the Middle East," begins the president. "Good news at last, I'm pleased to see."

"I'm afraid not," replies the National Security Advisor, sombrely.

"You don't think the peace negotiations will work out?"

"Err ... No, Madam President, the peace negotiations are going unexpectedly well," replies the National Security Advisor, somewhat confused.

"You're confusing me," replies the president, now a little irritated.

"Indeed, I'm a little confused myself. Before you appointed me I understood that you wanted to follow the Middle Eastern policy of your predecessor."

"Precisely, Dick. Peace and prosperity: that's what he was pursuing."

"Yes ... yes, he was. Peace and prosperity for the American people, Madam President."

"I was talking about peace and prosperity in the Middle East," replies Hilary Poinswatter, a little more exasperated.

"Err ... well, peace and prosperity for the American people doesn't always mean peace and prosperity for everyone else, especially in the Middle East. And, I must confess, I was under the impression that by now you would be fully aware of your predecessors' policies in the region."

"Well, of course I am. I was Secretary of State, remember," she replies with a touch of tetchy sarcasm.

"Err ... Well, clearly, you're not. You see, during my time as deputy director at the CIB President Rush decided that it was in our best interests to keep the Middle East conflict simmering away, as did his successor, and as did President Strumpet as well. None of your predecessors informed their Secretaries of State. Frankly, I'm surprised that you weren't informed when you assumed office."

"You're joking, of course," replies a stony-faced Hilary Poinswatter, unamused at the National Security Advisor's poor taste in what she believes to be his sense of humour.

"I'm afraid not. The ill-conceived intervention in the region by President Rush cost the US taxpayer three trillion dollars, and that's without paying the interest on the bonds we had to issue to finance

98

the war in the first place, I'm sure you're aware of that. President Rush and, later, President Strumpet, agreed that we needed to find a way of recovering those costs."

"Are you telling me that that the war in the Middle East has been deliberately encouraged to make money?" she asks, with a mixture of incredulity and scepticism.

"All four wars in the region, in fact, Madam President. Look, I appreciate that this is something of a shock, but we need to get our money back. And you must admit that we could have wasted three trillion more efficiently, rather than on pointless interventions that lacked legitimacy and only succeeded in pissing everybody off."

"Really? On what?" Her reply is rhetorical, and not intended to elicit a considered reply. Rather, it is intended to convey her disbelief and displeasure.

Failing to comprehend her true sentiments Richard Head replies, "Well ... err ... Like every sane person, I view universal healthcare as unchristian. But at least we'd have got some sort of return if we'd wasted three trillion on that, not to mention the thanks of at least a few citizens."

"Are you serious?" booms the president. Richard Head's face loses some of its colour.

"Err ... about free health care?" he replies a touch nervously.

"No. About the wars!" she yells. She is still sceptical, and goes on by saying, "If everything you've been telling me is true, why have we been financing and arming the moderate rebels, if not to bring about an end to hostilities?"

"Well, obviously, Madam President, we can't have the American people believing that its government is deceitful and duplicitous even though it is ... err, in fact, deceitful and duplicitous. The people need to believe that its government is doing everything to see that the good guys win – not that there are any good guys in reality. They're all mindless, bloodthirsty psychopaths, intent on carnage."

"So who is it that we've spent two billion dollars arming and equipping?"

"Well … err, in truth … no one. At least not many," he replies anxiously.

"What do you mean?" she asks, narrowing her eyes and fixing the National Security Advisor with a forbidding stare.

Richard Head twists his head sideways and feels his collar.

"You must understand, Madam President, that none of what I'm about to tell you had anything to do with me … at least, I wasn't directly responsible."

"Go on," she says sternly.

"The so-called five thousand moderate rebels never really existed. They were largely a myth created by the War Department and the Central Intelligence Bureau. In fact the last contingent suffered catastrophic casualties only last month—"

"How many?" interrupts Hilary Poinswatter.

"Five—"

An aghast Hilary Poinswatter interrupts once more.

"Five hundred?"

"Err, no. Five. Apparently these five men became extremely intoxicated one evening, took their armoured personnel carrier out for a joyride, drove over one of their own anti-tank mines, and blew themselves up. I'm afraid that's the end of the moderate rebels."

Hilary Poinswatter's head drops and she lets out a deep sigh.

"This would be scandalous if it were made public. But at least it means the peace process can go ahead."

"You mean to say you're *actually* in favour of peace?"

"Of course. Dick, we can't squander any more money on what you yourself said are pointless and illegitimate foreign interventions."

The National Security Advisor lets out a deep sigh, removes his spectacles, and begins to clean their lenses.

"Madam President, China owns about 25 per cent of our country. Hell, if they didn't lend us the money to buy their goods in the first place our economy would grind to a halt. If things don't change, in thirty or forty years a slant-eye will be sitting behind your desk in this office."

"How is this relevant to the matter at hand?"

"We need these wars not just for economic growth, but for our economic survival. Do you realise that hundreds of thousands of jobs in the Defence Sector rely *directly* on continued conflict worldwide, and millions more indirectly? Not to mention the very healthy tax receipts to the Treasury from the defence corporations.

"Allowing the peace process to continue will eventually see an end to *all* four wars that are raging in the region. The consequences could be catastrophic. You won't be popular if tens of thousands of people are made jobless almost instantly," replies Richard Head.

Hilary Poinswatter stands up, walks to the windows, folds her arms in contemplation, and gazes out on to the White House grounds. As a former corporate lawyer she has never been inclined or disposed towards a principled and moral viewpoint. Nevertheless, she is struck by a sense of unease and a feeling of uncharacteristic indecisiveness.

On sensing her unease and indecision the National Security Advisor interrupts her thoughts in order to press the issue.

"The elimination of the moderate rebels ... I'm afraid there's more."

"What do you mean?" replies the president as she turns to face her advisor.

"We can't account for the two billion dollars that they received."

****

It is late afternoon in Moscow and early morning in Buenos Aires. Poota Bastardo is on the phone to the Russian president.

"Mrs Pushkin, I am extremely concerned that your plan has not taken into account the reaction of the Americans, during and after our reconquest of the Malvinas."

Vladimira Pushkin sighs with boredom.

"Dear Poota, I can only assume that you have been indulging in too much of your own product, as you appear to be the only person in the world who is unaware of Hilary Poinswatter's complete contempt for Berkeley Hunt."

"I'm sure that President Poinswatter is still embarrassed by events at Buckingham Palace a year ago, but I do not believe that her personal animosity towards Berkeley Hunt will diminish her country's historic ties with the British. After all, the Americans provided the British with considerable assistance the last time we tried to recapture the Malvinas. Let us not forget that they have been allies for over a hundred years and have fought in six wars together. They have a very special relationship," replies the Argentinian president tartly.

Vladimira Pushkin allows herself a hollow laugh and says, "I see that you require something of a history lesson and an education in political realities. Do you know why the Americans intervened in what we in Russia call the 'Great Patriotic War'?"

"Of course," she replies, tetchily, resenting what she perceives to be the Russian president's condescension. "To save Britain and Europe from falling to Fascism."

"Indeed," begins Vladimira Pushkin. "That is certainly the *perceived* wisdom, which is taught to American and European schoolchildren. However, at the time many influential and powerful Americans were barely concerned about Fascism. In fact, many were sympathetic towards it.

"In reality the American political establishment had two considerably higher priorities than defeating it. Number two was to contain Communism. But by far the biggest priority was to bring about the collapse of an institution that was not only loathed by the

102

majority of the American people, but was also a large impediment to implementing American hegemony of the Western world: the British Empire. This was a task in which the Americans succeeded admirably. The method of its execution impresses even me."

"Impresses you … How so?"

"By becoming their ally rather than their enemy, the Americans were able to impose crippling financial conditions and covenants on the British, such that the post-war economic environment was so abysmal that the Empire's demise became inevitable," replies the Russian president.

"I suggest that you are misguided. The Americans provided the British with considerable economic aid," replies Poota Bastardo, who is becoming a little bored with the lecture.

"A myth. It was simply propaganda to bolster the image of capitalist America as benevolent and selfless. The British paid through the nose for this assistance – a heavy economic cost indeed, suffered by the ordinary British people, to be sure. Do not forget either that, by becoming so emasculated, the British were forced into becoming the Americans' *fidus Achates*. – doing the Americans' bidding when instructed …"

"*Fidus Achates*?"

"It has come to mean, my dear Poota, 'loyal companion', like a pet dog. The British have been unable to escape their leash for seventy years. Do not overestimate their fondness for one another. Besides, Hilary Poinswatter has more pressing concerns in the Pacific with the Chinese, and soon she will have equally pressing concerns in the Atlantic with the North Koreans," replies the Russian president.

"This is all very interesting, but how can you guarantee that the Americans will not intervene?"

"Because in the *end* I have something that the Americans want. And, as Churchill was fond of saying, 'The Americans will do the right thing … in the *end.*' Certainly always, when it is in the interests of their government."

"What could they possibly want from you?"

"That is not your concern, Poota. But, rest assured, there will be no American interference with your plans."

"And the British … Can you guarantee that they will not reinforce the Malvinas? Because, should they do so, I cannot guarantee a successful invasion. In fact, I cannot even guarantee that my military will proceed with the operation."

"Trust me. They will not."

Poota Bastardo knows she needs to tread carefully. She is struggling not only to control but also to disguise the frustration in her voice.

"How can you be certain? Err, I mean … *Are* you certain?"

"Calm down, Poota. I *am* certain, in the same way I was certain about Primadonna. My agents will see to it that the islands are not reinforced."

****

"What do you mean, 'The two billion dollars can't be accounted for'?"

Hilary Poinswatter is stunned by this revelation as she moves back to sit down in her chair behind her desk.

"Well, some of it can – equipment and arms – but the majority of it has gone missing," replies Richard Head. Hilary Poinswatter is a little taken aback by her National Security Advisor's less than perturbed reply.

"That money," begins Hilary Poinswatter, "was funnelled through the Central Intelligence Bureau, the War Department, and the National Security Commission. You're in charge of the National Security Commission (the NSC), and you were previously

104

responsible for the budget of the CIB." Her eyes start narrowing with suspicion.

"The money was never funnelled through the CIB. I can prove that. When it was passed through the NSC my predecessor was in charge. I suspect that was the reason why he shot himself – he couldn't find the money, and was afraid he'd take the rap. His timing was poor, because we discovered just last week that a marine corps officer who sat on the executive of the commission, Brigadier General Oliver Southgate, embezzled a large amount that was passed through the NSC—"

"Why hasn't he been arrested?" interrupts the president, the incredulity and annoyance clearly evident in her voice.

"He's gone missing. Not even his wife and children know where he is. We're investigating, of course."

"You mean he didn't take his family with him?"

"Well, it appears that he preferred the ... err ... *company* of his adjutant. He's gone missing too ... aah ... Obviously we weren't aware of General Southgate's ... err ... proclivities, shall we say."

Hilary Poinswatter lets out a deep sigh and holds her head in her hands.

"This is going to cause a lot of trouble in the Senate when it gets out." She looks up, struck by a realisation. "Wait a minute ... Wasn't it Senator Gormmless's committee that was responsible for the oversight of the NSC?"

"Err ... yes."

"Well, everyone knew he was a senile old fool. And now ... well, he's dead. Problem solved. We'll just blame the whole thing on him," says Hilary Poinswatter, now a little more relaxed.

"Err ... well it's not that simple. To cover his tracks General Southgate routed some of the funds to the State Department through an accomplice at the department who, needless to say, has also gone missing."

The president's face loses some of its colour.

105

"Well, I had no knowledge of that," she replies, a tad defensively.

"I know, Madam President, but if it came out it would look very bad indeed. Hell, the scandal about your emails and use of a non-secure server would look like an overdue parking ticket in comparison."

Hilary Poinswatter fixes her National Security Advisor with a glacial stare.

"What do you advise?" she says, still regarding him coldly.

"Well, it might be possible to err … make the whole thing go away."

"Well, then do it," she replies curtly.

Richard Head pauses for a few seconds and then replies slowly and deliberately, "Aah … yes. Well, there's still the question of the Middle East. Perhaps we could discuss that first." He looks down and examines his fingernails.

Hilary Poinswatter's eyes narrow once more. The National Security Advisor feels their piercing glare bore into the top of his head.

"Are you trying to blackmail me, Dick?" she asks firmly.

"No, ma'am," he replies innocently. He is mindful of his desire to live up to the dissembling, disingenuous reputation of his former employer, the CIB, but is nonetheless uneasy about forcing the hand of his commander-in-chief. He continues forcefully, "Look, Madam President, peace in the Middle East would be a disaster, as I explained before. The economic consequences would be catastrophic."

Richard Head stands up and begins to pace the Oval Office.

"Like the majority of Americans, I didn't vote for President Strumpet when he was elected, and not just because he looked like an orangutan with a hairpiece. That said, putting America first … well, second – behind him, of course – was his priority. He was prepared to do whatever it took to preserve the superior moral standards and ethics of our great nation. If that meant, and means, the instigation and continuation of bloody conflict around the world, then it's a price worth paying to protect the American way of life and the principles upon which this country was founded, and for which it continues to stand."

Then, concluding with as much bluster as possible, he says, "It's a task that remains unfinished, and one that I am prepared to carry out."

"Nice speech, Dick, but the peace process is well underway and I don't see anything derailing it. Certainly Pushkin won't."

"There I believe you're wrong. We have something Pushkin wants," replies the National Security Advisor confidently, as he resumes his seat.

"I take it you mean Operation Grand Slam."

"Precisely. We allow her to execute Operation Grand Slam unopposed, and in return she derails the peace process and allows her clients to begin an offensive in the Middle East."

"Our NATA allies, particularly the Norwegians, are not going to be pleased about this."

"Well, we don't have to tell them," replies Richard Head quietly, while staring at down at his hands once more. He knows that he is committing his commander-in-chief to a dangerous – if not impeachment-worthy conspiracy, and has already worked out a way of ensuring that he remains completely blameless.

Hilary Poinswatter swivels her chair to face the windows and gazes in to the White House grounds once more. She is silent and reflective for a full minute before replying.

"Can we be certain that Pushkin will go for the deal?"

"Leave that to me," he replies.

"And the Arab nations … Aren't they exhausted by endless fighting?"

"Hell, no. They still believe they're in the Dark Ages. Slaughtering each other brutally and as viciously as possible to the

107

bitter end is what they live for. Hell, it's not just a religious duty. It's their most popular form of entertainment."

"What about our marines and air support in Norway? Pushkin won't believe us if they are still there."

"We'll remove them at the appropriate time, under the pretext that they are needed elsewhere – Poland, for example. That shouldn't arouse the suspicions of the Norwegians and the British. Without our marines and air support to back them up they'll just sit there and do nothing when Pushkin moves in to Finland."

Hilary Poinswatter turns to face Richard Head and says, "Supping with the Devil is a very dangerous business for *both* of us."

"I'll be sure to take a very long spoon. But there are other factors we need to consider about Operation Grand Slam."

"What now?" she replies with some frustration.

"The Argentinians," he replies.

****

It is early afternoon in London. As usual, after a heavy lunch, Berkeley Hunt is about to drift off to sleep behind his desk. His telephone rings. He yawns and answers it.

"Berkeley?" enquires the voice furtively, at the other end of the line.

"Yes?"

"It's me," the voice cautiously responds again.

"Who?"

"Me," says the voice once more, now almost in a whisper.

Berkeley Hunt is becoming irritated and says, "Look, speak up. I can barely hear you, for God's sake."

"It's me, Donald. Is this a secure line? Can you talk?"

"Err, yes, of course. What can I do for you, Donald?" enquires Berkeley Hunt, not really wanting to do anything for him at all. Donald Kaczka is the prime minister of Poland, and one of only two heads of government who are well-disposed towards the British prime minister. He is perhaps the *only* head of government who takes Berkeley Hunt seriously, which only underpins the British prime minister's view – and the view of everyone else – that Donald Kaczka is a raving, delusional paranoiac.

"I've had some information for some considerable time and, with all that has been going on in the last few days, I think you should be the first to know."

"Right. Well, what is it that I should know?" replies Berkeley Hunt, stifling a yawn. Donald Kaczka is well known for his outlandish hare-brained conspiracy theories, to which even the British prime minister does not give any credence.

"I am convinced now that Angela Bunt is a Russian agent, and that—"

"What, the Chancellor of Germany?" Berkeley Hunt can barely contain himself from bursting out laughing.

"Yes. There is some circumstantial evidence pointing to her being a member of the East German security police during the Communist period ..."

"Hold on a minute, Donald," begins Berkeley Hunt. The Chancellor of Germany is the only other head of government with whom Berkeley Hunt is on good terms, and so he is even more disinclined than usual to believe Donald Kaczka.

"Angela Bunt has been a staunch supporter of NATA. For goodness' sake, she's just agreed to reinforce your country with her troops."

"Precisely. That is why I'm worried, knowing that she is Pushkin's agent."

"With respect, Donald, I would like to remind you of certain other assertions that you have made. A year ago you swore that there had been a secret deal between President Strumpet and Pushkin, allowing her to annexe the Baltic States. Then you said that Pushkin had secretly funded Strumpet's election campaign and hacked his opponent's computer servers to ensure his ascendency to the presidency—"

Berkeley Hunt is interrupted by an almost apoplectic Polish prime minister shrieking, "But I am right. Don't you—"

"I haven't finished, Donald. A number of years ago, when you were a journalist, you wrote that there was a conspiracy being orchestrated by Muhammad El-Fatwad, the owner of the world's most exclusive department store, to overthrow the British monarchy. So, you see, you've got quite a lot of form in this area."

"Don't you see, though, Berkeley, that everything that has happened makes sense if you accept what I'm saying? Surely you don't believe that Bunt invited all those refugees from the Middle East out of compassion and humanity, do you?"

"Err ... Well, of course—"

"No! She did so on the orders of Pushkin, to create chaos and panic, and to sow the seeds of fear and mistrust in Central Europe – which is exactly what has occurred – not to mention destabilising the Western alliance," replies the Polish prime minister, his anger now reaching a zenith.

"Look ..." begins the British prime minister, sounding conciliatory in an attempt to calm down his opposite number, and then employing some half-baked psychology, which he once heard being debated by four women on a popular lunchtime TV programme.

"I know things have been a bit rough for you, what with all those foreigners piling up at your borders, but don't you see? You're simply blaming the cause of all your angst, animosity, and frustration on someone that you've never ever *really* liked."

"You're not listening, Berkeley! Operation Grand Slam ..."

"Exactly. Operation Grand Slam. You've hit the nail on the head. Pushkin is interested in Finland ..."

"That is disinformation. Operation Grand Slam is a deception plan. Pushkin's real target is me."

"You?" Berkeley Hunt almost laughs once more.

"I mean Poland. She wants to annexe us, not Finland. And with German troops on Polish soil, and with your troops having left, it will be that much easier."

Berkeley Hunt sighs. He has pretty much made up his mind to reinforce the Falken Islands with the British paratroopers moved by Admiral Turgidly from Poland to St Helen's Island, as he views it as the least worst option.

"I'm sorry, Donald, but I had no choice. Besides, it may only be for a few days or a couple of weeks at most."

"It'll be too late! The Russians will be here by then."

Continuing to be conciliatory, Berkeley Hunt replies, "Donald, you know that Great Britain will always guarantee the independence and security of Poland ..."

"You said that in 1939, so you'll understand if I do not feel particularly reassured," interrupts the Polish prime minister, with a large dose of unmistakable sarcasm.

The British prime minister is beginning to lose some of his composure.

"Be realistic, Donald. OK, let us assume that Angela Bunt *is* a Russian agent and that for years she has been passing classified documents to Pushkin. So Pushkin knows all our military plans for the defence of Eastern Europe. Even if she were to be arrested this second Pushkin would still know all our plans, which we can't exactly change in five minutes. What is she going to get her troops to do? Attack your soldiers?"

"Exactly."

Now somewhat vexed, Berkeley Hunt says, "For God's sake, Donald, the Krauts aren't the mindless goons they were seventy years ago. Bunt's officers simply won't obey those orders, because they will think she's gone stark raving mad."

The Polish prime minister's paranoia gets the better of him.

"What if her officers are also involved in this conspiracy?"

111

"Look, I've got to do what I've got to do. When you speak to that old cow Poinswatter I think you'll find that she will agree with me," replies the British prime minister, a slightly harder edge in his tone.

"Why? She hates you. I'm sure you haven't forgotten what you did to her at Buckingham—"

"I wish people would stop bringing that up!" replies Berkeley Hunt, who is now becoming more than a little irritated.

"Poinswatter will agree with me *and* support NATA's decision to help you with German troops. You know I'm right." Berkeley Hunt knows nothing of the sort, but is trying everything to get the Polish prime minister to back down.

The Polish prime minister sighs.

"Yes ... I fear that you are," he replies, now somewhat resigned to the inevitable.

"There you go," says Berkeley Hunt jovially. "Great minds think alike."

"Or fools seldom differ," replies Donald Kaczka caustically, as he hangs up the phone.

****

Back at the White House ...

"The Argentinians? I take it you mean Bastardo's plan to capture the Malvinas," says Hilary Poinswatter.

"Err ... you mean the Falkens, but yes," replies Richard Head.

"Well, that's the one bit of good news I've had all week. Losing the Malvinas will certainly put another nail in the coffin of that idiot Berkeley Hunt – maybe the final nail, with luck."

"It would be far from good, Madam President. I appreciate that Berkeley Hunt did not exactly endear himself to you, due to the unfortunate incident last year at Buckingham Palace—"

Hilary Poinswatter interrupts her National Security Advisor and fixes him with a scolding stare.

112

"I do not appreciate being reminded of that, thank you very much, Dick."

"Err … yes, of course," replies Richard Head contritely.

Hilary Poinswatter continues, "Anyway, what difference does it make if the Malvinas are in Argentine hands? Since we are striking a deal with Pushkin, it makes no difference if British Forces remain in the European theatre or are redeployed to recapture the islands."

"Not quite, Madam President. If the Falkens are captured by Bastardo, then in order to recapture them the British will need to despatch their entire fleet as well as most of their ground forces in Europe. The Russian flotilla in the South Atlantic would return, and would have almost unchallenged control of the Baltic. Europe would be dangerously exposed to any other hostile moves that Pushkin may contemplate."

"What other hostile moves? You're just speculating."

"Perhaps, but hear me out on this point. As you know, the Drug Enforcement Bureau suspect Bastardo of being one of the world's biggest cocaine smugglers. Were the Falkens to fall to her she could use the islands to expand her base of operations to export cocaine on a massive scale. Obviously, as there would be no benefit to the US government, we can't allow such a brazenly criminal activity to go unchecked."

"OK, Dick, that's a fair point …"

"But there's more, Madam President. Whether Bastardo wins or loses against the British, I'm sure Pushkin will have her eliminated and try to have her replaced with a puppet leader. The Russians will then have an even stronger foothold in Latin America. Once she finds out about it Pushkin may even take over Bastardo's cocaine smuggling business. If Bastardo successfully retakes the Falkens it would be much harder for us to engineer a government sympathetic to the US, even though she would be dead.

"On the other hand, if Bastardo fails there will most likely be a coup and we may be able to install a government more aligned to our interests. In short, the British must not only be allowed to defend the Falkens but they must also absolutely be held, no matter how much you personally hate the British and Berkeley Hunt."

"Can the British do so without significant troop withdrawals from Europe?" enquires the US president.

"I understand, from the head of the UK Joint Intelligence Committee, that two days ago Berkeley Hunt approved the redeployment of paratroopers from Poland to their bases on St Helen's Island, on twelve hours' standby. Fortunately, the Chancellor of Germany has agreed to support the defence of Poland with German troops, which should deter Pushkin from any hostile moves in that direction. So yes, I think the British can stop an invasion without degrading Eastern European defences."

"Good. When do you intend to contact Pushkin?"

"Later on today, Madam President. I'll do it from here, if I may."

****

It is early evening in London. Berkeley Hunt is admiring a painting in the library of his brother's Belgravia home.

"I didn't know you liked Picasso?"

"I don't," replies Mike Hunt, as he passes his brother a drink. "And that's a particularly ghastly example, in my view."

"Then why did you buy it?" exclaims an astounded Berkeley Hunt.

"Because next year some new-moneyed oik, with pretensions to taste and harbouring ambitions of climbing the social ladder, will give me three million more than I paid for it."

Berkeley Hunt shakes his head.

"I haven't seen Ruth in a while. Do you know where she is, by the way?" he asks, referring to their younger sister.

"She's in Istanbul, softening up some potential clients for me. Oh, yes, before I forget," says Mike Hunt as he reaches into his inside jacket pocket. "Give this to Lafarge, will you? Tell him it's from me," as he passes his brother an envelope.

"What is it?" enquires the younger Hunt, as he reaches out.

"Five hundred thousand pounds in bearer bonds."

"What?" exclaims Berkeley Hunt, dropping the envelope, now even more astounded and not a little confused. "I don't get it. One minute you're blackmailing him. The next you're giving him money. And, anyway, it's not like you to put your hand in your pocket."

"You're right. I didn't put my hand in my pocket. Several weeks ago I persuaded the big bean counters, the big shysters, and the mandarins at the tax office to put their hands in theirs. I told them it was in their best interests if they wanted to keep tax reform well away from Parliament."

"And they believed you?"

"Of course. Five hundred thousand is petty cash to them, and now that the bill has been booted out by Parliament they're more than delighted."

Naturally, Mike Hunt has signally failed to mention that he actually received one million pounds in total from the large accountancy and law firms and the civil servants' union.

"Hold on a minute, Bruiser. It didn't cost you anything to get the bill squashed, so why give anything to Lafarge?" asks Berkeley Hunt.

"Because, right this minute, Lafarge is probably hatching some little plan to get back at me. The five hundred thousand is rather like a box of chocolates, a sort of 'thank you for your help'. You know what a hothead he can be, so the money will heal his bruised ego and will calm him down. Being in a more rational state of mind he'll think twice about crossing me."

"I don't know how you can abide that man, Bruiser. He's a complete thug. If only I could get rid of him. He makes Australians look civilised."

"He has his uses. And, besides, his long list of misdemeanours will keep him off my back and come in handy in ensuring that HM Government does what's right," replies Mike Hunt.

"Let me guess ... what's right for Goldstein Brothers, for big business, and for any other bugger with a ten-digit bank balance.

"I don't know why I bother doing this job. I don't know why we bother having democratic elections when everything people vote for is quietly pushed to one side by you and your mates," replies Berkeley Hunt both wearily and with some sarcasm.

After handing his brother another drink Mike Hunt sighs deeply before replying. He fails to detect the sarcasm.

"I'm really not surprised that you only got a pass at philosophy and politics, Humpty. You know, at the time I told Father that the backhander of three million quid to get you into Oxford would have been better spent on bribing a US senator ..."

"Three million?"

"What?" snaps Mike Hunt, irritated by the interruption.

"You said three million? Why did you take out five million from my trust fund when Father died, then?" asks Berkeley Hunt.

"Did I say three? Well I meant five," lies Mike Hunt, and continues, "Anyway, stop interrupting. Why do you think there are revolutions, civil war, and insurgencies happening in the Middle East? "

"For once, Bruiser I think I know more about what's going on over there than you do. I get daily updates from the military and from expert political analysts."

"Expert political analysis ... ha! Stuff and nonsense. Go on, then Humpty. This should be interesting," replies Mike Hunt with more than a little scepticism.

"Err ... Well, the way I see it is that the Arabs have got a bit sick and tired of being run by dictatorships, and then there are the religious dictatorships that they're also sick and tired of. So the whole thing's just ended up in one massive great punch-up between the people who just want to be left alone to live freely, the dictators who want to continue dictating, and the religious dictators who want to replace the – well … the other dictators."

"Not bad, Humpty, not bad. But you have completely missed the real reasons as to *why* … the whole thing's a bugger's muddle in the first place."

"I thought I'd summed it up rather well, actually," replies Berkeley Hunt, slightly peeved.

"It's not because they're dictatorships that the Arabs are in revolt, it is because they are quite *obviously* dictatorships. Even the plebs in the Middle East recognise when they're being shafted.

"Now our plebs, here in Blighty and in the West, are a lot more savvy. We haven't been able to blatantly pull the wool over their eyes for over a hundred years. They woke up in the end when, for absolutely no reason whatsoever, millions of them were slaughtered in the Great War.

"It was then that the plebs finally twigged the real reasons why their betters had been sending them out for centuries to be skewered at the end of a lance and blasted by shot and shell. Not for patriotism, but to thin out the ranks of the plebs and ensure that their masters could continue to enjoy their rightful privileges. Well, it was touch and go for a while, what with the advent of Communism and socialism. Our class almost bought the farm. The all-encompassing education system didn't help, either …"

"What's wrong with a decent education system?" asks a slightly aghast Berkeley Hunt.

"Well, it didn't seem to do a lot of good to you, did it? And yours was particularly expensive: three – err, five – million quid plus. But anyway, you're interrupting, and we're digressing.

"Well, to keep the plebs in line in the West we've had to be a bit more innovative and subtle. Enter, stage left, twentieth-century democracy, a concept totally divorced from its ancient roots. The modern brand of democracy – or so-called democracy, Humpty – has existed for decades to precisely achieve the very opposite of what the masses believe it exists to do. It's there to confuse people into believing that they have a real say in how they are governed and that they have freedom and rights, when in fact they have little of either. This has been achieved in a rather subtle way ..."

****

It is late evening in Moscow. Vladimira Pushkin stands gazing out of the French windows in her office on to the city below. The ever-present Kronsteen stands silently by the side of her desk. There is a knock on her door.

"Come in," instructs the Russian president. The general from the previous meeting enters, approaches Pushkin, and stands patiently waiting for an acknowledgement. She turns and accepts the file that he has brought with him. Her telephone rings and she walks purposefully back to her desk, gesturing to the general to follow.

She presses the loudspeaker button.

"Good evening, Mrs Pushkin."

"Good afternoon, Mr Head. Sooner or later I expected you to call," replies the Russian president, taking her seat.

"In which case we can dispense with the small talk. Do we have a deal?"

"Of course."

"Good. I'll advise the president to withdraw our ground forces from Norway and redeploy them to Poland, as well—"

"I don't think so," interrupts Vladimira Pushkin firmly.

"What do you mean?" replies the US National Security Advisor, with some irritation.

"Do not insult my intelligence, Mr Head. From Poland it would only take you six hours to redeploy your troops back to Norway."

"Why would we want to do that? We'd be breaking our end of the deal."

"Mr Head, once I reignite the conflict in the Middle East not even I will be able to stop it. I'm sure you're aware that my clients in the region are more than eager to continue slaughtering their brethren to the bitter end. It should be obvious to you that, with respect to our arrangement, I would be at something of a disadvantage. Restarting a war in the Middle East that I cannot stop would allow you to abrogate your side of the bargain."

Richard Head is silent and reflective for a few moments. Although he shares many of the traits of previous US National Security Advisors, being strategically short-sighted and dogmatically narrow-minded, he is not a complete idiot. He strongly suspects that the Russian president has ulterior motives behind her objection, but is unable to fathom what these might be.

"A compromise, Mrs Pushkin. We'll withdraw our forces to Italy," he says.

"Spain," she replies assertively.

"Agreed. One last thing. I want you to call off Bastardo. She is not – repeat – not to invade the Falkens," says the National Security Advisor.

"What makes you think I exercise that amount of influence with President Bastardo?"

"It is now *you* … who are insulting *my* intelligence, Mrs Pushkin," replies Richard Head, the disdain clearly apparent in his voice.

"Very well. I cannot guarantee that the Argentine president will heed my recommendation but, as we both know, the British are at this moment planning to significantly reinforce the Falkens. In those circumstances I can categorically assure you that the Argentine military will not risk a confrontation with the British," she replies.

Although he is not convinced about Vladimira Pushkin's bona fides, the National Security Advisor knows he is unable to assert his country's interests any further.

"Well, I think we have an arrangement," he says.

"Good. I will send you a timetable tomorrow that will detail our move against Finland and the resumption of hostilities in the Middle East. Goodbye, Mr Head," she replies.

"Goodbye, Mrs Pushkin," says Richard Head as he disconnects the line.

"Well, what do you think?" ask Hilary Poinswatter, looking up at Richard Head from her desk, as he stands looking out on to the White House lawn.

"I don't think she'll renege on our deal on Finland and the Middle East. But, unless the British reinforce the Falkens, then I'm sure that she'll force Bastardo to invade. You need, as a matter of urgency, to tell the British prime minister that he needs to reinforce the islands immediately."

The US president shudders.

"Oh, God, must I? Can't you just inform their chiefs of staff?"

"Of course, but unless the British prime minister is pressed by you personally it may not do any good."

Hilary Poinswatter stands up and begins to pace up and down for a few seconds. The prospect of speaking with Berkeley Hunt three times in the same month is almost as abhorrent as the thought of intimate conjugal relations with her husband. Sighing, she replies,

"Very well."

****

"Esoteric obfuscation," says Mike Hunt, lighting a small cheroot.

"What?" replies Berkeley Hunt, clearly mystified.

"Precisely. Confusing, isn't it? The art of political concealment. Ensuring that what is obscure appears to be transparent, when it is in fact unfathomably opaque – rather like camouflage," replies Mike Hunt smugly.

"I'm still not with you, Bruiser."

"I didn't think you would be. As I said, the purpose of twentieth-century and twenty-first century democracy is to confuse the plebs. We can't be too blatant, of course. Some of them are quite intelligent and well-educated."

Mike Hunt takes a drag of his small cheroot and continues. "The way that this has been achieved is to litter our domestic and international legal framework, local by-laws, regulations, and directives, with a series of undecidable propositions."

Berkeley Hunt scratches his head and looks even more puzzled, "Err ... still not sure I'm with you."

"A statement which can be proved to be both true and false simultaneously, so if we want an outcome to be either true or false that's as good as done. We always win. We can't win all the time, of course. That would demoralise the plebs and make them suspicious. So we throw them a bone now and again."

"What sort of a bone?"

"The easiest way to think about it, Humpty, is to imagine society as a man with a very long tapeworm inside his guts. The man ingests water, food, and vitamins, but it is the tapeworm that absorbs most of the nutrients provided by this nourishment. Obviously it can't take *all* the nutrients. The man would die and, subsequently, so would the tapeworm ..."

"I'm not really following your analogy, Bruiser."

"Stop interrupting and I'll explain. Now, the man is society: more accurately, the plebs. The tapeworm is so-called democracy. So-called democracy sucks just enough out of the man to keep him in a state bordering on exhaustion. Thus he is disinclined to question the complexities and the machinations of the system in which he lives.

"The man (the plebs) gets thrown a bone from time to time in the form of cheap money, artificially created economic booms, and the right not to allow the construction of public toilets, car parks and motorways – that sort of thing. This makes them feel content for a time and fosters the impression that they have some influence in how society is governed.

"The really important decisions, due to esoteric obfuscation, are taken by us, the Establishment. Obviously if the plebs realised that they were being played and manipulated there'd be bloody revolution. Think of so-called democracy as a game of chess – where one player is a grandmaster and his opponent is someone who doesn't even understand the rules, let alone the strategy.

"Democracy, Humpty, is nothing more than an elaborate charade that has been designed to ensure that the haves continue to have and that the have-nots remain oblivious to that fact."

"You know, Bruiser, I'm almost inclined to believe you, except for one crucial cornerstone of real democracy.

"Really? What would that be?" replies Mike Hunt, with a mixture of boredom and scepticism.

"Well … the free market. You know, ordinary people making decisions freely and taking risks in order to reap financial rewards."

Mike Hunt bursts out laughing.

"The free market … Oh dear, oh dear. Don't make me laugh, Humpty."

After a few moments his laughter subsides. He sighs and continues, "The free market doesn't really exist. Well, not in its purest sense. Every time a large bank or insurance company is about to collapse, or the automobile industry looks as though it's going tits up, guess what? They get bailed out – by the taxpayer, no less.

"Stimulus packages … an even bigger laugh. They're nothing more than the plebs borrowing money from themselves, and having to pay the interest on the debt to someone else.

"Then there's quantitative easing: just a rather subtle way of robbing the plebs' pension funds. So what does all that tell you?"

"Err … Well, governments need to maintain financial stability, even though it might be painful in the short run."

"Not exactly. What this state of affairs tells you, Humpty, is that the owners of capital – capitalists – retain most of the upside economic potential with virtually none of the downside risk. While the plebs – the taxpayer – has almost none of the upside potential and almost all of the downside risk. The free market exists when it is convenient for capitalists to allow it to exist."

"I'm still not sure, Bruiser. I think maybe … you're being overly cynical."

"Really?" replies Mike Hunt caustically. "Tell me, what is it you think we *actually* do at Davos every year?"

"I wouldn't know. You've always stopped me from going," replies his brother sulkily.

"Well, of course I have. It's one thing for the French president to be photographed cavorting with a lap dancer and getting spanked. That's par for the course for a Frog statesman, and something that wouldn't surprise anyone. But it's quite another matter for a British prime minister to be so compromised. And, knowing you, Humpty, you wouldn't be able resist the temptation. After all, I wouldn't want someone else to have a hold over you. Besides I suspect HM Treasury would baulk at the thought of the million dollars per head entry fee—"

"A million dollars … I didn't think it was that much," interrupts Berkeley Hunt.

"Of course. A regiment of call girls, gigolos, and half a ton of cocaine aren't cheap, you know. Anyway, contrary to popular belief, we don't get together to solve the world's economic problems …"

"Well, what do you do, then?"

"We endeavour, Humpty, to maintain the status quo. We battle to prevent the equitable distribution of wealth. That's the *real* agenda."

Berkeley Hunt is becoming increasingly perplexed. His initial sarcastic outburst and assertion earlier that evening about the relevance of democracy were born out of frustration and cynicism, rather than any real conviction to his stated point of view. However,

123

he is now beginning to suspect that there might be some truth to his brother's claims. He desperately begins to grasp at straws in the hope that Mike Hunt may be wrong.

"Well, what about the Brexit vote, eh? You didn't see that act of popular defiance against the political establishment coming, did you?"

"I'll tell you what, Humpty, I'll give you that one. But it's really not that significant, otherwise I wouldn't have bothered twisting Dave's arm into offering the referendum in the first place—"

"Then why did you do it?" interrupts an astounded Berkeley Hunt.

"Well, Lafarge offered me a very lucrative opportunity. He had some very sensitive financial information that would turn a large profit, and offered to share it with me if I could persuade Dave to offer a referendum. Needless to say, I agreed."

"I don't know why Dave didn't stand up to you." Berkeley Hunt's reply is not so much a question but is rather a statement of wistful regret, which his brother fails to detect.

"Really, Humpty? Have you forgotten how I and the other prefects used to lock him in the sock bin for an hour each day, and then, for good measure, give him a diarrhoeal bog wash? Well, after that, the mere sight of me used to send him into an awful funk. So, when both I *and* Lafarge turned up on his doorstep, he practically had a heart attack.

"Anyway, by the time all the Is are dotted and all the Ts are crossed for Brexit half the people who voted for it will be dead, and the other half will have forgotten what the whole thing was about in the first place. I think you'll find that the final terms for Brexit, when it's all done and dusted, will be no different to the terms that we accepted when we were full members of the European Community. The irony, of course, is that most people won't even notice."

"Well ... well, maybe you're right," replies the prime minister, peevishly. "But it doesn't detract from the fact that the people spoke and made their views clear and showed that they were prepared to take a stand." He says this while puffing his chest out in an attempted show of defiance.

"Indeed, Humpty, it'll be a very fine pyrrhic victory," remarks Mike Hunt drily.

"But it wasn't just Brexit that was a big wake-up call to the Establishment, was it?" begins Berkeley Hunt. "I mean, even if you think nothing will change after Brexit there's still this rising tide of populism ... and nothing showed that more than the election of Donald Strumpet to the White House. How do you explain that, eh?" he concludes with an unusual amount of assertiveness.

Mike Hunt takes a long drag of his small cheroot, exhales, gulps down the last of his drink, and then replies as though lecturing a schoolboy.

"Humpty, when there's a drought and people are dying of thirst they'll drink anyone's piss, even if it comes from a diseased, narcissistic megalomaniac. In fact, *especially* when it comes from a narcissistic megalomaniac."

"Well, you say that, but how do you explain the fact that Strumpet remained popular with the ordinary voter throughout his presidency?"

"The man was a game show host, a reality television star, a celebrity. For centuries, Humpty, religion was the opiate of the masses: the unadulterated worship of unseen, unfathomable deities. Today that has been replaced by celebrity worship – the unadulterated adulation given to ubiquitous, gibbering, witless nonentities, who excel at being vacuous and vainglorious at the same time.

"Strumpet understood this better than most and was able to create a loyal fan base out of these celebrity-worshipping halfwits, and thus create a power base as a consequence. The tackier, the tawdrier – and the more tasteless – he became, the more his supporters adored him, because the more he reminded them of their own false gods. In the end I suppose we really have to thank Strumpet. He kept celebrity worship not just alive and well, but encouraged it."

"Hold on a minute, Bruiser. One minute you're scathing about so-called celebrity worship. The next … well, you're praising Strumpet for keeping it going. I don't get it."

"For us, the Establishment, celebrity worship has been something of a godsend. It has distracted the plebs – and, more importantly, their children – from focusing on what is important and what is truly relevant to improving their lot. The plebs today are far more interested in the inane ludicrous opinions and proselytising of some barely literate and wholly inarticulate pop culture icon. It's far less taxing intellectually for the plebs to allow themselves to be taken in by that sort of nonsense than for them to focus a few brains cells on reasoned concepts and the sort of intelligent, rational argument that might actually be of some benefit to them.

"Of course there is a potential downside to celebrity worship. If the plebs continue to listen to the mind-numbing and incoherent babbling of their idols, their brains may atrophy to such a degree and their IQs collapse ... they will cease to become productive, and so be unable to make us – the wealthy – wealthier."

Berkeley Hunt scratches his chin, as though in deep contemplation. "You know, I sort of take your point about the celebrity bit, and I'll admit Strumpet wasn't my cup of tea. But his policies were aimed at improving the lives of the ordinary American. That much is certain."

"What is certain, Humpty, is that he threw a few crumbs at the American plebs – which they gratefully received – while enriching himself and his extended family. By the time he left the White House he and his family were ten times as wealthy. You know, I have a sneaking admiration for the old lecher. He came from nowhere – had no breeding. His German grandfather worked as a sausage maker, and his mother came from the bogs of Ireland.

"You've got to hand it to him. He achieved the highest office in the land – indeed the world – and kept his hand in the till for all that time without getting nicked. Admirable, really."

"How the hell do you know that?" asks Berkeley Hunt incredulously.

"Know what?"

"That he had his hand in the till. And why wasn't he nicked?"

"Do you really think that he reversed climate change policy because he didn't believe in the science? Of course not. No, he was taking considerable sums in backhanders from the oil companies and the rest of the fossil fuels industry. Believe me, I should know. Goldstein Brothers manage that money. As for Strumpet never getting nicked … Well, when you have backhanders on an industrial scale it reflects rather badly on your form of government. It doesn't help anyone to have that sort of thing exposed.

"Anyway, I think I've educated you enough for one day. So, anything happening with the Argies?"

****

Vladimira Pushkin has just finished her telephone conversation with US National Security Advisor Richard Head. She picks up the phone once more and dials a number.

"Good evening, dear lady."

"Good evening, Madam President," replies the voice at the other end of the line.

"I trust that all your planning for Operation Grand Slam has now been completed," says the Russian president.

"Indeed, Madam President. We are ready to proceed, once you give the order," replies the voice at the other end of the line.

"Excellent. How will you neutralise the enemy forces before they can engage my ground troops?" enquires the Russian president.

"As you know, two of my senior commanders are former agents of yours. They have already informed lower-echelon commanders that our host's military has been infiltrated by Russian agents.

"The lower-echelon commanders have orders to seize key infrastructure and communications facilities, as well as military command and control centres, upon the commencement of Operation Grand Slam.

"The enemy troops will be neutralised and disarmed on the basis that Russian fifth columnists have infiltrated their ranks. Prime Minster Kaczka will be informed accordingly. But, before he has time to react, your forces will already have entered the country and taken control of the rest of the Polish military facilities."

"Excellent. You have done extremely well. I look forward to meeting you in Warsaw, Chancellor Bunt."

Vladimira Pushkin puts down the phone.

The Russian general has been waiting patiently for Vladimira Pushkin to finish her calls, as he has a particular reservation that he wishes to express to his commander-in-chief.

"Why are you still here, General?" asks the Russian president, somewhat brusquely.

The general begins to perspire slightly.

"Err … well, I have some concerns, Madam President …"

"About what?" Again Vladimira Pushkin's tone is somewhat abrupt.

"Is it absolutely necessary to proceed with our South Atlantic operation?"

"Of course—"

The general boldly interrupts the president. "I am concerned that a significant number of our naval forces will be out of position. Our South Atlantic flotilla could be more effectively employed in the Baltic or the North Cape, should the Americans renege on our arrangement—"

Vladimira Pushkin interrupts herself and replies in an almost scolding tone, "Clearly you have not been paying attention, General. The Americans have as much to lose as we do, should they renege."

"Perhaps, Madam President, but I really don't understand the nature of our strategic objective in our South Atlantic operation."

"That is why you are a general, General, and I am the president." Vladimira Pushkin calms down, exhales deeply, and pushes herself back into her chair. She continues in a more genial manner.

"Please sit, General," she says, "and I will explain." The general takes a seat.

The Russian president begins. "The Americans believe that, if Bastardo is successful in capturing the Falkens, Russia will have even greater influence in Argentina and South America in general. They probably suspect that we will eliminate Bastardo, whatever the outcome.

"However, they believe that if Bastardo loses against the British then they, the Americans, will be able to influence any future Argentine government once she is no more. They will undoubtedly press the British to heavily reinforce the Falkens and so bring about her demise, when her naval and ground forces are defeated."

"I agree, but it seems to me that the Americans are correct. Should Bastardo fail in her attempt at conquest, Madam President, they will be in a position to influence the next Argentinian government."

"Not so, General. The Americans are unaware that we too are cognisant of Bastardo's criminal activities and, unlike them, are in possession of the evidence in that regard—"

"Forgive the interruption, Madam President, but why bother to compel Bastardo to invade the Falkens at all? Why not just make her criminal activities known to the Argentine people and then subvert her regime?"

"Compelling Bastardo to invade the Falkens was necessary, in order to expedite the withdrawal of as many British troops and aircraft as possible from Poland, General. I had calculated — correctly, that upon detecting the threat to the Falkens, the British would move troops from Poland to St Helen's Island. Naturally, this would increase the probability of successfully executing Operation Grand Slam smoothly.

"Yes ... yes, of course," replies the general, feeling a little foolish. "But what if the British *do* in fact reinforce the Falkens? We both know that the Argentine military would be reluctant to carry out an invasion."

"The Falkens will *not* ... be reinforced, I have already seen to it. Berkeley Hunt will thus be forced to deploy his submarines to prevent an invasion."

"Do you think Berkeley Hunt would really attack a fleet on the open sea in international waters?" asks the general.

"Ultimately, he will have no choice if he wishes to retain control of the Falkens. Losing the islands would be his ruin. It is all part of my plan, General. The inevitable destruction of the Argentinian fleet by British submarines will bring about the downfall of Poota Bastardo. Once we have eliminated her, and her criminal conduct has been laid bare by our puppet, his credibility and bona fides will have been truly established. And he will have cemented his place as their new dictator – under our guidance, of course."

The general is still a little baffled.

"Indeed, but may I ask what value there is in controlling the government of Argentina? They are virtually bankrupt."

"General, we have made a very significant investment in that country, which we need to recover. You are right. As a financial risk we would have been better off lending that money to Greece. By assuming control of Bastardo's narcotics operation we shall be able to do precisely that: recover our investment."

"Very clever, Madam President," replies the general admiringly.

"There's more, General. By controlling Bastardo's drugs empire we will be able to flood the North American continent, and more precisely the United States, with cheap and plentiful cocaine. In five years' time the minds of the current crop of American youth will have become so addled that, by the time they are eligible to vote, installing any sort of government we wish will be even easier than it was for us to ensure the election of Donald Strumpet to the presidency."

"An excellent plan, Madam President."

"I know," replies Vladimira Pushkin, matter-of-factly.

****

Back in the library of Mike Hunt's Belgravia home, Berkeley Hunt stands up, exhales deeply, runs a hand through his unruly hair, and makes his way to the drinks cabinet to refresh his drink.

"Well, it's not looking good, Bruiser. The Argies look as though they really are going for the Falkens."

"Excellent. About time we had a good punch-up."

"What? You can't be serious. Good God, even a small war will create panic on the world stage. What with the North Koreans roaming about with their nuclear subs, backed up by the Chinese, it's making the South Koreans and the Japanese very twitchy. Then there's the Russians playing silly buggers in Europe."

"Humpty, there's nothing like a good old-fashioned war to boost economic growth. We learnt that after World War Two. America wouldn't be what it is today, had the last war not happened."

"I don't see how a relatively small war in the South Atlantic is going to boost economic growth. If anything, what with everything else going on, it seems to me that a war with the Argies will create panic on the financial markets."

"It'll boost economic growth if the fighting becomes contagious and drags in other combatants. But, anyway, well done, you're catching on. Financial chaos, panic, and confusion are perfect ingredients in making large amounts of cash."

"I thought you financial chaps don't like uncertainty."

"We don't. But, if one is aware of an impending disaster before it occurs, one can profit from it very handsomely."

"For goodness' sake, Bruiser, don't you have enough money? I mean you could buy ... well ... Greece, if you wanted."

"Humpty, my gardener could buy Greece. Besides, I was thinking more on the lines of ... aah ... Jamaica. And one can *never* have enough money. Now, what are you going to do about the Argies?"

"Well, with all the other potential flashpoints around the globe, I don't think the Cabinet and the chiefs of staff want to start a war ... not if it can be avoided. So I thought I'd reinforce the islands with paratroopers and fighter bombers. That'll dissuade them, I'm sure."

"Dissuade them ..." Mike Hunt almost explodes. He calms down and continues in a more conciliatory manner.

"Now look, don't you want to go down in history as one of our greatest prime ministers?"

"Err ... well, didn't want the job in the first place, as you know, so I'm not sure I care that much."

Mike Hunt is careful to keep his temper under control.

"Think about it Humpty," he says, putting an arm around Berkeley Hunt and pretending that he actually gives a fig about his younger brother. He gestures towards the window and out into space.

"In fifty years' time people could be talking about you in the same hallowed way as they do today about Maggie, Winston, and the Iron Duke. Just imagine: you could be 'Sir Humpt ... err ... Berkeley Hunt', or 'Lord Hunt', the marquess or duke of somewhere or other. Think what that would mean for your grandchildren, eh?"

"Well ... err ... knowing me, I'd probably forget where I was marquess or duke of. But, anyway, I don't think that's going to happen. I mean, I don't think it'll matter whatever I do, as most of the country loathes me."

"Precisely, Humpty: most of the country loathes you. But all is not lost. All you need is something big and dramatic to reverse your fortunes."

"Such as what?" Once again Berkeley Hunt is slow on the uptake.

"Well, you remember when Maggie came into power, she was dreadfully unpopular ... and then she had a remarkable stroke of luck with the Argies invading the islands. Well, after they got a good thrashing, Maggie could do no wrong in the eyes of the people forever thereafter."

"Let me get this straight, Bruiser. Are you suggesting that I should *allow* the Argies to invade the Falkens, so that we have a full-on war with them?"

"Precisely," replies his brother, rather smugly.

"Well ... err, if I just reinforce the islands no one need get killed, and I'll look like a strong and decisive leader."

"Indeed Humpty, and everyone will have forgotten about it in a week. No, what you need to take your place in history is a really big punch-up with a few dozen mangled dead bodies on display. *That* ... is something people *won't* forget."

"But what if we lose? A few dozen mangled British dead bodies isn't going to do me much good then, is it? Good God, I'd probably have to leave the country. The people would go from loathing me to wanting me strung up!"

"He either fears his fate too much, or his desserts are small," replies Mike Hunt, who deliberately refrains from completing the quotation:

"...Who dare not put it to the touch
To win or lose it all."

—Field Marshal Montgomery, June 1944. Abridged from The Marquess of Montrose, the Battle of Edgehill, 1642.

"What?" asks his brother, bewilderment clearly showing on his facc.

"Never mind. The point is that if you want the big pay-off, sometimes you have to take the big punt."

"But I don't want the big pay-off. I don't care about the big pay-off.

"Bloody hell, I don't even want to do this job. I'm sorry, Bruiser, but I won't do it."

Berkeley Hunt finally wakes up to his brother's real motivation in trying to manipulate him into starting a war.

"Blackmailing me to torpedo the tax reform bill is one thing. But I won't send hundreds – maybe thousands – of men to their deaths so that you, no doubt, can make a few quid. That's what you really want.

"I don't care if you threaten me with those photos and I have to resign. I don't even care if you threaten to tie up my trust fund, because at the least I'll have my prime ministerial pension to live on."

Mike Hunt lights another small cheroot and moves over to the mantelpiece, where he rests his elbow. He eyes his brother coolly and begins.

"You know, many years ago I was having a conversation with Father …" Somewhat uncharacteristically, Mike Hunt suddenly becomes bleary-eyed and nostalgic.

"He said he recognised in me the qualities that would take our family to even greater heights. Even as a sprog he said I was 'a proper little Hunt'. He was proud of me for never getting caught for all the misdemeanours I'd committed.

"And then he talked about you. He couldn't understand how you turned out the way you did. He told me that he could only conclude that Mama had been rogered senseless by the gardener or the chauffeur or the gamekeeper. Or maybe all three."

Berkeley Hunt's eyes widen and his jaw drops.

Mike Hunt takes another drag of his cheroot and continues, "In spite of his suspicions about your provenance, Humpty – or lack of, I should say, Father was deeply concerned about you. He said it wasn't the fact that you were a half-witted, weak and vacillating indecisive fool that concerned him, but rather this absurd compulsion of yours to do the right thing and please everyone. It would all end in tears for you if it wasn't nipped in the bud.

"He said if it weren't for this flaw in your character you'd easily manage like most other well-bred public school failures, by defrauding an insurance company or two or embezzling a few elderly wealthy widows. But, since you are what you are, you'd probably end up on the street.

"His dying wish, Humpty, was that I look after you and guide your every decision," lies Mike Hunt as he wipes away an imaginary tear from his eye and feigns heartfelt sentiment.

"Oh, leave it out, Bruiser. You've been bullying and blackmailing me my whole life," replies Berkeley Hunt, surprised by his own audacity.

"True enough, but it was for your own good, Humpty. Where would you be today if it weren't for me, eh? I arranged for you to be an MP, then Foreign Secretary, and now prime minister—"

"Precisely," Berkeley Hunt interrupts angrily. "I wouldn't be prime minister, and I wouldn't have to put up with all this bollocks and all the other bollocks that I've had to for the last year, if it weren't for you."

Mike Hunt's tone hardens.

"So I take it that you're adamant about reinforcing the Falkens, and nothing will change your mind?"

"Exactly," replies his brother, sounding surprisingly assured.

"You're sure?"

"Look, Bruiser, you can blackmail me all you like with those photos and my trust fund. My mind is made up."

"Very noble, Humpty. And yes, I thought pushing you into starting a war of your own volition may be a step too far. But,

135

anyway, I wasn't going to blackmail you with the photos or your trust fund."

"You weren't?" replies Berkeley Hunt, more than a little surprised and quite confused.

"No. I knew it would be insufficient leverage. But I have something far worse."

"What?" Berkeley Hunt is at first alarmed, and then regains his composure. "I don't believe you. I know there's nothing I've done that could embarrass me more than those photos."

"Indeed, certainly not wittingly. But unwittingly you've committed a rather serious crime."

"What do you mean?" replies Berkeley Hunt, now a little less confident.

"Remember that dago chappie, the ex-footballer who got killed in a plane crash a couple weeks ago … Franco Primadonna?"

"What about him?"

"Well, he was something of a drugs kingpin, and …"

"What has that got to do with me?" asks Berkeley Hunt, becoming ever more confused.

"If you're quiet and listen, I'll tell you. Two years ago Franco Primadonna deposited ten million dollars at the Caribbean branch of Goldstein Brothers. The branch exists specifically to handle the business of less reputable and more unsavoury individuals.

"Primadonna had decided to give up his life of crime and had agreed to testify against his boss, who apparently had accrued a staggering forty billion dollars …"

"Who was his boss?" enquires the prime minister.

"That doesn't matter. Now shut up. In exchange for his testimony Primadonna was to be granted immunity from prosecution and political asylum in a country of his choice. Well, the Americans didn't want him, so we, HM Government, that is, agreed to take him on certain conditions …"

"Bruiser, I don't remember any of this, and I *was* Foreign Secretary at the time."

"Of course you don't remember, because you were never told. The whole thing was kept hush-hush between the prime minister's office and the party chairman, and of course the party chairman informed me. It was agreed that Primadonna could have political asylum and leave to remain in the UK under an assumed identity in exchange for a consideration."

"Let me guess ... the ten million that Goldstein Brothers were holding for him," says Berkeley Hunt, in an unusually insightful piece of deduction.

"Precisely. Now the PM didn't really like the idea, what with her father having been a bishop and all that, so only agreed if the money were given to a charity for war widows and orphans.

"The party chairman, on the other hand, being a practical and pragmatic fellow, who didn't have a soppy clergyman for a father, realised that the money could be far better utilised by the party.

"I'm not sure how he did it, but I suspect Primadonna was getting desperate, and the PM was more concerned with the Brexit hullabaloo and having to keep one eye on Lafarge as her deputy. However, the party chairman managed to persuade them to allow the transfer of the ten million into the party's bank account—"

"I still fail to see how this has anything to do with me ... Money being moved from here to there, of which I had no knowledge, and which in any event appears to be entirely legitimate," interrupts Berkeley Hunt, who is now become a little weary.

"I'm getting there, Humpty. I'm not sure how the party chairman was going to keep the money in the party, but that problem was partly solved by the PM popping her clogs. So the only people who knew about the origin of the money were the party chairman, me, and Primadonna ... and, as you know, Primadonna bought the farm about two weeks ago.

"A few days ago you, as party leader, signed a document authorising the retention of those monies for the benefit of the party."

"No I didn't. I have no recollection of doing anything of the sort," replies Berkeley Hunt, in something of a protesting tone.

"I'm afraid you did, Humpty. When I came to see you at No.10 four days ago, the document was amongst the papers given to me by the party chairman for your signature. I knew you'd sign it as you never bother to read documents requiring your signature – never have as I recall."

Mike Hunt walks over to the bureau on the other side of the library, opens a drawer, and removes a document. He walks back towards his brother and hands him the piece of paper.

"This is a copy of the document that you signed, Humpty. The original is under lock and key at the party headquarters."

Berkeley Hunt examines the document.

"All right, I signed the document. So what?" replies Berkeley Hunt, sounding unconcerned. "The whole arrangement was approved by my predecessor and the party chairman, so what have I got to worry about?"

"There is no official documentation whatsoever signed by either the late prime minister nor the party chairman approving or authorising the party to receive and use those funds for the benefit of the party. The only document that exists is Primadonna's authorisation to Goldstein Brothers to transfer that money to the party's bank account, to be used however the party sees fit. And I'm pretty certain that, to cover himself, the party chairman has a document from the late PM instructing him to use those monies for charity."

Berkeley Hunt is starting to feel a little less comfortable and is beginning to clasp at straws.

"OK, but Primadonna was granted immunity from prosecution in return for his cooperation … which means that I still have nothing to

138

worry about because the money he gave the party is just part of a wider arrangement, presumably with the knowledge and approval of the law enforcement agencies."

"I'm afraid not, Humpty. Any immunity he may have been promised was conditional upon him testifying against his boss. Well, Primadonna's dead: ergo, no immunity. Which means that you approved the receipt of funds for the benefit of the party from a self-confessed drug smuggler."

Berkeley Hunt's pale, pasty face begins to turn even paler.

"Now *I* know that you are innocent," begins Mike Hunt, "and that you had no idea about the provenance of the money, nor that it even existed. But I'm not so sure that a court of law will come to the same conclusion.

"Then there's the Americans. They take a pretty dim view of drug smuggling and money laundering. After what you did to that Poinswatter woman at Buckingham Palace I'm sure she'd rub her hands gleefully at the thought of getting her claws into you on the other side of the pond."

"Oh, God, you're not wrong. She would, as well," says Berkeley Hunt, in a state bordering on panic.

"Most certainly. If you end up in chokey over there, they'll be able to drive a juggernaut through your pooper by the time those hillbilly convicts have finished with you. You know how they love fat pasty white boys. Oh, yes, and when you are finally released you'll be totally penniless. Your trust fund will be swallowed up by fines, penalties, legal fees ... that sort of thing.

"No prime ministerial pension for a convicted felon I'm afraid. You'll end up living on a council estate in some dreadful northern town, where you'll have to learn to speak Urdu or Punjabi or some other foreign language. And, if she hasn't divorced you by then, you'll probably have to put your wife on the game, as I doubt anyone will give you a job, so much as shovelling manure."

Mike Hunt pauses for a few moments to allow the severity of his brother's predicament to sink in, and then continues. "So what's it to be, eh, Humpty, old boy? Everlasting glory ... or bird and buggery?"

Berkeley Hunt stares in wide and wild-eyed terror at the cold, ruthless expression on his brother's face.

****

"Ow!" squeals Berkeley Hunt.

"Stop squealing, stop moving, and stop being such a big baby," scolds Penny.

"Well, it hurt. Ow," he squeals once again.

"There ... that's the last one," says Penny as she removes the last splinter of wood from Berkeley Hunt's left buttock. She opens a bottle of liquid ointment and splashes it over Berkeley Hunt's rear end. And then, with a cloth, she gently dabs and then rubs the liquid into his skin.

Berkeley Hunt sighs with relief. As Penny finishes he turns over gingerly on to his back. Penny joins him on the bed and continues in a scolding manner.

"What's got into you, Berkeley? You've never asked me to thrash you with a piece of four by two before ... and do you know how difficult it is to get a plank of wood at this time of the evening in Bayswater?"

"Sorry, Penny dear. It's just been one of those days." They are both silent for a few moments.

"Well, go on," she says, a little irked by Berkeley Hunt's refusal to break the silence.

"What do you mean?"

"Berkeley, don't play games with me. I've known you long enough. I've never seen you as tense and stressed as this."

Berkeley Hunt slowly blows out his cheeks, such that his lips vibrate, and then replies, "I'm in a real pickle, Penny."

140

"What sort of a pickle?"

"Bruiser's got me over a barrel."

"What does he want this time?"

"Well, if I don't let the Argies invade the Falkens *tout de suite*, he'll see to it that I end up in chokey with a bunch of homo hillbilly homicidal hombres across the pond. And that old bag Poinswatter will be there looking to throw away the key."

"That sounds just like him. Why don't you let him have his way if it'll keep him quiet?"

"Penny, love, it'll mean war ... hundreds, maybe thousands of men will die if we have a full-scale war right now. No ... I've got to work out a way of, well ... sort of starting a war so that Bruiser makes a few hundred million that he doesn't need ... I don't end up doing bird, and no one actually gets killed, at least no one on our side. It's perplexing, I can tell you," says Berkeley Hunt, sounding perplexed.

"You know, Berkeley, I've noticed that your brother and other rich toffs are always angry and dissatisfied. And do you know why that is?"

"Haven't a clue," replies Berkeley Hunt, too fatigued and stressed to realise that the question is rhetorical.

"It's because they know that they'll be sharing the same fate as the lowliest human being on the planet, no matter how much money they've got. They'll be pushing up daisies just like the rest of us and they'll be thinking that's unjust, because rich people think they deserve something better. So because they don't, in the end, get anything better, they are nasty and mean and spiteful to everybody else."

Berkeley Hunt blows out his cheeks once more and replies, "Penny dear, you've become quite the philosopher. I'm sure if you keep this up your tutor will give you a first."

"Do you think so, Berkeley? That's very nice of you. Professor Hawksworth said the very same thing about me not long ago."

"Hawksworth? The Oxford cosmologist who won the Nobel Prize?" asks Berkeley Hunt incredulously.

"Oh, yes. Do you know him?"

"Of course I know him. Everybody on the planet knows him!"

"He's such a sweetie. Pops down from Oxford every month for his usual. You know, I don't charge him anymore. Most of the time we just sit about talking about, life, the universe, and everything, for hours and hours. It's such an education for me.

"Here, would like to see a photo?" Penny opens a bedside drawer, removes a photo frame, and shows it to Berkeley Hunt. The photo is of Penny kissing a bespectacled man on the cheek, who has a wide grin and is sitting in a motorised wheelchair.

Berkeley Hunt stares at the photo and then quite puzzled, shakes his head.

Day Twenty-Three

"Right, I've made up my mind," says Berkeley Hunt, trying to project as much authority into his voice as he can. He is addressing a COMA meeting in the Cabinet Room at Number 10. It is morning.

"We're going to leave the paratroopers and fighter bombers on St Helen's Island."

"What? You're not going to defend the islands?" replies an astonished Nick Lafarge.

"Of course I am," replies Berkeley Hunt, "I just don't want to antagonise the Argies and have them accuse us of militarising the islands and escalating the situation."

"What do you mean, 'escalating the situation'? How could it be any more escalated than it already is?" asks Nick Lafarge, with some degree of annoyance and incredulity.

"All right, suppose we reinforce the islands and the Argies still invade. Dozens or maybe hundreds of people will get killed—"

Interrupting him, Nick Lafarge says casually, "Well, they're only bloody Argies."

"No! They won't just be Argies, they'll be our boys as well. That's why, Admiral, I want you to send in both our submarines on a war footing to intercept and destroy their fleet, if it looks like they are going to invade."

"I'm afraid, Prime Minister," replies Admiral Turgidly, sounding quite uneasy, as he is not convinced about the merits of Berkeley Hunt's strategy, "that we only have one submarine on patrol in the area. HMS *Ariadne* has had to be withdrawn, due to problems with its reactor core, which means that it is unable to stay submerged for any length of time. The nearest other attack submarine is nearly five thousand miles away, so it won't get there in time. HMS *Argo* is the only boat we have on station."

"Right ... Well, it'll have to do the job on its own, then, won't it?" replies the prime minister, in an unexpectedly assertive tone.

Sir Percy Talleewacker, the Cabinet Secretary, sensing Admiral Turgidly's unease, interjects.

"Prime Minister, we can't just go around blowing foreign warships out of the water in international seas."

"Of course we can, if they're going to invade our sovereign territory," replies Berkeley Hunt.

"With respect, Prime Minister," begins Sir Percy, "we know that they're probably going to invade. So do the Americans. And obviously the Argentinians and the Russians know they are. But the rest of the world doesn't. The Argentinians could argue quite reasonably that they were conducting naval exercises with their Russian friends in international waters when they were on the receiving end of an unprovoked attack by the Royal Navy. We would be severely reprimanded in the UN."

"Prime Minister, the safest course of action would be to reinforce the islands with our paratroopers and fighter bombers from St Helen's," says Admiral Turgidly.

"No," replies Berkeley Hunt, almost shouting the instruction. On realising that he is making something of a spectacle of himself, and possibly arousing some suspicion, he continues in a more measured tone.

"Look, I just don't want there to be even the slightest chance of British casualties. That can be assured by using the submarines to stop an invasion."

Admiral Turgidly takes a deep breath and then replies, "Prime Minister, I am *absolutely* certain that, if we were to reinforce the islands, the Argentinians would not launch an invasion."

"How can you possibly know that?" retorts the prime minister with more than a little scepticism.

"We have a high-level informant in the Argentine administration."

"Well, who is it?" asks Berkeley Hunt.

"I'm afraid I can't tell you, Prime Minister," replies the admiral.

"What? I'm the prime minister, for God's sake!"

"I appreciate that, sir, but the informant is extremely nervous and contacted us very recently, in a rather roundabout fashion, to ensure that their identity was not discovered. The individual doesn't want any details to be revealed to anyone other than those who were originally contacted, and me."

"So you're asking me to take a decision based upon an informant of whom I have no knowledge and whose bona fides cannot be verified? I'm sorry, Admiral, but it's not good enough," replies the prime minister.

Under normal circumstances Berkeley Hunt would in all probability accept Admiral Turgidly's recommendation. But, mindful that his brother is holding him by the short and curlies, he is doing everything to rationalise his way out of making the right decision.

"Prime Minister," begins Admiral Turgidly, "I'm sure you are aware by now that not only will the Argentine and Russian fleets be in the area, but a North Korean fleet will shortly be passing between the islands and the Argentine mainland. The Americans have despatched a carrier group to monitor them …"

"Bloody hell. Dagos, Russkies, Gooks, and Yanks. Getting a bit crowded down there, isn't it?" exclaims Nick Lafarge.

"Precisely, Deputy Prime Minister," says the admiral, with some alarm in his voice. "Things could soon escalate if there's an incident. It's possible that our submarine could accidentally attack and sink a

Russian warship, and we would therefore be in a virtual state of war with them."

Berkeley Hunt holds his head in his hands and slowly blows out his cheeks.

"Well, perhaps we could attack the Argies once they enter our territorial waters?"

"Not possible. Our submarines cannot operate within fifty miles of the islands, as the waters are not only too shallow but there is also an increased chance of them being detected. Their main weapons system, the Javelin sea-skimming missile, has a maximum range of thirty miles. So the invasion fleet would be well out of range when it's in the islands' territorial waters," replies the admiral.

Berkeley Hunt blows out his cheeks once again and replies, "Well, it looks as though we've got no choice, then. We're going to have to attack the Argies on the open sea."

"Have you gone mad, Hunt?" asks Nick Lafarge. "Haven't you been listening to Sir Percy and the admiral? Hold on a minute … Didn't I hear you speaking to Poinswatter earlier this morning? What did she have to say?" he enquires suspiciously.

"Yes, I was, and she said that it was imperative that we defend and hold the islands, which is what I'm doing. Now, I've given you my reasons – twice. That's the end of it!

"Admiral, order HMS *Argo* to intercept and destroy the Argentine invasion fleet as close to the Falkens' territorial waters as possible."

Admiral Turgidly sighs.

"Very well, Prime Minister. I should point out that with only the one submarine we may not be able to intercept the enemy fleet and thus stop the invasion. In those circumstances – and if there is the political will – we will need to assemble a large task force, probably the entire navy, to be able to recapture the islands. As I pointed out before, we will need to borrow an aircraft carrier from the French … so I respectfully suggest that you contact the French president."

"Oh, very well. I don't really want to speak to that drunken lecher, but if I must, I must. Anyway, I think you're all being a bit too pessimistic. If worst comes to the worst, I can always threaten to nuke Buenos Aires. That'll get Poota Bastardo thinking twice," says Berkeley Hunt, laughing.

****

It is early afternoon in Moscow. Vladimira Pushkin is standing in front of the French windows in her office, soaking up the late spring sunshine. Her telephone rings. Distracted from her reverie, she makes her way back to her desk, sits down, and answers the phone.

"Hello, Mira, you sexy minx. How are your plans for world domination going? Oh, yes ... and, by the way, do you still have that husband of yours chained up in the basement?" asks the voice at the other end of the line.

The Russian president smiles inwardly and outwardly laughs. Not even Kronsteen, her bodyguard and lover, would dare to address her with such familiarity, but she feels almost attracted to her British agent for his keen and intelligent mind and recognises in him a kindred spirit.

"Oh, my goodness," she jests. "I forgot I left him there, and that was three months ago," she laughs. Although she is probably the most dangerous woman on Planet Earth her laugh is rather engaging, and is one of the reasons why her British agent is attracted to her.

"Never mind," he replies. "You can always feed what remains of him to the crocodiles in your dungeon."

Vladimira Pushkin laughs once more and then asks, "Is it true that you have been subpoenaed to give evidence at the trial of Silas Munchkin?"

"Good news travels fast, doesn't it?" he replies with a touch of dry sarcasm. "I'm afraid it is. I did everything to try and get out of it... even thought about trying to bribe the US Attorney General, but decided that would be counterproductive. Now, if it had been Donald Strumpet's Attorney General, he would have taken a pay-off in the blink of an eye."

"Do you think that Munchkin was running his human trafficking and slavery business while he was at Goldstein Brothers?" she enquires.

"Good Lord, no. That would have been far too risky."

"Yes but he got caught anyway," remarks the Russian president wryly.

"True enough, Mira, sweetheart. But, as US Secretary of State for Commerce in Strumpet's government, he was in rather the perfect position to pull it off. I'm sure Strumpet looked the other way and took his cut. Munchkin probably made close to a couple of billion dollars out of the venture. I have to say I'm almost jealous."

"A couple of billion … That much?"

"Of course. Think about it. It's not a capital-intensive business but it *is* a high-margin one. After all, you don't need to pay slaves, so of course he made a fortune. Ironic, really, when you think about it, what with Munchkin having been a banker."

"What do you mean?"

"Banking wouldn't be as big and as important as it is today had it not financed slavery for more than two hundred years. And don't forget: even in your own country serfs were bought and sold through letters of credit, and so on."

"Not that I care particularly, but I am nonetheless intrigued, as the process of American justice has always fascinated me … What do you think will become of Munchkin?" asks the Russian president.

"Justice? The American courts don't exist to dispense justice. Well, unless you define justice as going to prison for the rest of your life just for being black. No, Mira, darling, the American court system exists to cut deals. It's really quite efficient: plea bargains … that type of thing. The more deals the court system makes the better the conviction rate statistics look. Don't forget the amount of money that the Department for Justice rakes in every year from alleged miscreants of all types. And of course, there's the quota system for prisons, ensuring that they remain crammed to the rafters with convicts, so that the private security firms can maximise their profits – at the taxpayers' expense, no less. American justice ... it's a well-oiled business.

"So the worst outcome for Munchkin? He'll end up paying a fine of two hundred million dollars *and* stay out of prison, to boot. On the other hand, if he is fortunate and gets the right judge and jury ... Well, at worst, bribing them will only cost about fifty million. It would be more expensive than a British court of course – the British don't value justice quite as highly – but it's still a pretty decent bargain."

"I think I prefer my brand of justice."

"Yes, I bet you do," replies the British agent drily, and then continues.

"Oh, yes, I always keep meaning to ask you ... Is it true that there was a porcupine in that video of Strumpet in the Moscow hotel room, as well as the donkey and the gerbil?"

She laughs and asks, "Why is it that people always ask about the existence of a porcupine, and barely mention the donkey or the gerbil?"

"So it's true, then. The video *does* exist?"

"I never said that. I just don't understand what people think you can do with a porcupine."

"Well, the fact people don't ask about the other two is easily explained. Strumpet always harboured ambitions of becoming a Hollywood bigwig. A donkey is fairly standard deviant debauchery for Hollywood actors, directors, and producers. Now, if it was Strumpet himself who made the video, then maybe he was trying to impress them.

"The gerbil is a bit of an acquired or specialised deviancy, generally favoured by those Hollywood types who convert to

Buddhism or that nonsensical Scientology rubbish. But I must admit that I don't really get the porcupine either. So does the video exist?" asks the British agent.

"Even between friends certain things must remain secret, I'm afraid."

"Oh, well, you can't blame me for trying."

"Indeed, and it's been nice having this little chat. Now to business," says the Russian president, her tone becoming more businesslike.

"Certainly. Everything that you have asked me to do I have accomplished," replies the British agent.

"You're sure there is no possibility of the position being reversed, or any other setback?"

"*Absolutely* not. I guarantee that everything will be just the way it is. I wouldn't say so otherwise."

"Good. I really would *not* … like to terminate our friendship if anything should go wrong," replies the Russian president. Although the intent is unmistakably threatening, her tone remains amiable.

"You really are a deliciously devilishly wicked wench. That's why I like you. Don't fret. Everything will be tickety-boo. So there now just remains the question of payment. Two hundred and fifty million dollars, I think we agreed, to my Caribbean account. You have the details," says the British agent.

"Of course. Tell me, is there *anything* you wouldn't do for money?" she asks.

"Most definitely. I'd be more than happy to come over there and give you a good gallop, and not charge you a penny."

Laughing once more, Vladimira Pushkin replies, "Of course. By all means please do come."

"Really?" replies the British agent, more than pleasantly surprised.

"Yes, if you can get past Kronsteen."

"Good God. Is that gorilla still working for you?"

"Indeed he is. He is proficient in *many* different ways."

"All right, then, as long as I can bring three gorillas of my own with me."

"That wouldn't be very sporting," she replies with mock disapproval.

"No one has *ever* accused me of being sporting. It's not in my nature. Besides, I earn my living by ensuring the odds are decidedly in my favour."

"Yes, I know you do. Come to Moscow anyhow. It would be nice to see you again, and your trip wouldn't be entirely wasted. I'm sure you remember my predecessor remarking that Russian prostitutes are the best in the world, so you may be pleasantly surprised and entertained while you're here."

"Yes ... and he should have known. When he wasn't running your country into the ground he spent most of his time banging the brasses. Anyway, I never pay for anything unless I absolutely have to."

"Yes, of that I am sure. You know, in this uncertain world the one certainty is that profit will always take precedence over patriotism for men of your profession."

"Comforting to know, isn't it? Besides, patriotism is the last refuge of the scoundrel."

"And I doubt that there is a bigger scoundrel than you. The two hundred and fifty million will be in your account by the end of the day. It was good to speak with you, Mike."

"And you, Mira, darling. And don't worry. The Falkens won't be reinforced. Ta-ta." Mike Hunt puts down his phone.

He stands up from his desk, looks skywards, and stretches out his arms exultantly. Then he claps his hands together and rubs them gleefully, a broad grin on his face. There is a knock on his door.

"Come in," he says.

Johnny Dangerfield, chief financial analyst for Goldstein Brothers Europe, enters the room.

151

"Have you suddenly become a contrarian?" he asks.

Johnny Dangerfield is in his early thirties and, having attended the same public school as Mike and Berkeley Hunt, albeit a number of years later, was personally selected by the former for his current position. He is highly intelligent, with a first-class degree in mathematics from a top university.

Johnny is tall and handsome, with an athletic physique, and he prides himself on spending several hours every week in the gym. In spite of his seven figure salary – not including bonuses, he lives beyond his means due to his fondness for Italian sports cars, top of the range speedboats, and the large mortgage on his smart London address.

Many women of a certain type find him very attractive, and indeed he boasts to friends and colleagues of keeping them on yo-yos attached to every one of his fingers. With his tall and confident bearing, he is often mistaken for an officer in the Grenadier Guards. However, in common with most Goldstein Brothers executives, and unlike a Guards officer, the thought of leading men into battle and exposing his person to danger would cause his hair to turn white and his boxer shorts brown. Johnny Dangerfield is man with a larger-than-life personality, and with character no larger than the head of a pin.

"What do you mean?" asks Mike Hunt.

"Your recommendations to our clients ... Buy sterling and sell gold?"

"And?" replies Mike Hunt brusquely.

"It goes against a lot of the technical and fundamental indicators. Gold: strong uptrend, increasing volume, and price rate of change, not to mention falling production. Sterling: well that's flatlining and, in all likelihood, there'll be another interest rate cut.

"And if that Canadian cretin at the Bank of England keeps printing money faster than the Chinese use toilet paper ... well, in a couple of years sterling will be practically worthless."

152

"Well, I can't disagree with you on the last point, old boy. The only difference between quantitative easing and counterfeiting is that you get nicked and banged up for counterfeiting. But, anyway, I wasn't thinking about a two year horizon … more like three to six months."

"And gold?" asks Johnny Dangerfield.

"Now look, Johnny, I can't tell you *all* the secrets my brother tells me."

"Your brother? Good God. Apart from some village idiot in Wales, everyone knows that he's a halfwit. As for the Chancellor … Well … he's still using an abacus because he can't work out how to operate a calculator, let alone a computer. I'm sorry, Mike, but I'm not convinced."

"Really? No matter. As head of this department the clients will accept my recommendations."

"I'm not so sure, Mike. If I query your recommendations with the other partners and set out the reasons in the department *and* client bulletin … well, there'll be questions for you to answer. I'm sure you don't want to tell everyone that your recommendations are based on insider information," replies Johnny Dangerfield confidently.

Mike Hunt goes back to his desk, sits down, leans back in his chair, and lights a small cheroot. He stares dispassionately at his protégé as he blows out smoke. He eyes him analytically, then asks, "So what do you propose?"

"Well, you're up to something. I don't particularly care what it is, but I'm certain that you wouldn't be doing it unless you stood to make at least a billion dollars. A hundred million my way tomorrow and I'll keep schtum."

"Ha," scoffs Mike Hunt. "Ten million."

"Can't retire on ten million, I'm afraid. Fifty, or no deal."

Mike Hunt continues to eye the younger man coldly. He realises that he hasn't much time to execute his plan, and so concedes.

"Fifty it is, then. Just make sure you keep schtum, otherwise something *very* unpleasant may occur."

"Of course. I'm not about to make trouble for myself. Send the money here," replies Johnny Dangerfield, as he passes his mentor a note.

"You know, Johnny, I'm surprised at you. In ten years you'd be a partner, with a much bigger remuneration package, *and* the opportunity to take advantage of the clients big time. So what's got into you?"

"Ten years is a long way off, and to tell you the truth I'm getting a bit bored and tired of the early mornings and late nights. It's playing havoc with my social and love life."

"So what will you do with your fifty million?"

"I thought I'd go to Nassau."

"Good Lord. Why do you want to go there? It's full of Americans, and not even the right sort. Just plebeians with money."

"Precisely. They're the most impressionable, and their daughters swoon at the sight and sound of a good-looking, well-dressed Brit with a plummy accent."

"Well, I suppose there is that. I have to say, Johnny, I always knew you'd grow into a first-class shit. That's why I hired you. But you forgot the first rule of investment banking. It's the clients you're supposed to shaft, not your colleagues, and *certainly* … not your mentor!"

"Rules are meant to be broken. Anyway, got to go Mike. Packing to do, I think," replies Johnny Dangerfield, laughing as he leaves the room.

Mike Hunt, gritting his teeth, exhales slowly. He is a little annoyed at having been got the better of to the tune of fifty million dollars. However, he soon calms down, and his normally ruthless and calculating demeanour returns. He changes the SIM card in his smartphone and dials a number. The call is answered by a male Indian voice.

"Mumbai Personal Services Incorporated ... Rundi Chode speaking. How may I help you?"

"Rundi, you old pimp, how's the brothel doing?" enquires the investment banker.

"Hello, Mr Mike ... Very well indeed. We have many Middle Eastern clients now and they have most unusual requests, so I am charging much, much more."

"Good for you. Now, I'm sending you the new access codes to the trading facility for the Caribbean account. This—"

"Betting against your clients again, boss?"

Sensing a cheeky grin behind the remark, Mike Hunt replies in a rebuking tone.

"Hold your tongue, chai wallah (tea boy). When I've cleaned up this time you'll be able to buy all the brothels in Bombay with your whack. Now this is what I want you to do: sell sterling and buy gold, and this is when and how I want you to do it ..."

****

It is early afternoon at Number 10 Downing Street. Berkeley Hunt and Nick Lafarge are once again sitting in the Cabinet Room. Nick Lafarge is reading his favourite tabloid newspaper. Berkeley Hunt is about to telephone the French president.

"I don't believe it. Have you read this?"

"What's the matter now, Nick?" asks Berkeley Hunt, sighing and putting down the phone. The deputy prime minister looks up from his newspaper.

"That Kiwi Communist, KY cavalier..."

"Who?" asks Berkeley Hunt.

"Satchell!" he replies angrily. "He wants designated cottaging zones in the Houses of Parliament. He says it's discrimination, and an infringement of his human rights, not to be allowed adequate facilities to engage in practices peculiar to his sexual orientation.

Orientation, my foot. Deviation, more likely. If I were prime minister I'd have him shot."

"No doubt you'd have me shot as well."

"That would be a waste of a bullet. I'd have *you* garrotted."

"Thanks. Right, now shut up. I've got to phone Molière, and frankly I'd rather have my teeth pulled out through my rear end."

François Molière is in his mid fifties. He is short, with receding dark hair and thick-rimmed spectacles. He is the most unpopular French leader since the chap who had his head chopped off.

Molière is sitting in a Jacuzzi with his friend and one-time political mentor and former president of the Italian republic, Salvatore Berlosconti. They are in the latter's private bordello on the island of Capri. A number of scantily dressed young women are milling around in the background, giggling and drinking champagne.

Molière has long since been treated with suspicion by the French electorate, partly for his heretical views on marital etiquette. Unlike the majority of Frenchmen, he refuses to retain the traditional – indeed – obligatory mistress that French society demands of its married men. Not that he cares about the sensibilities of his wife, he simply prefers to 'be more generous with his amorous talents to a broader range of females', as he described it. Once accused of drugging a woman, he was acquitted unanimously by a jury comprised entirely of men – French men, who agreed with his argument that it was perfectly reasonable to drug a woman *after* coitus to avoid having to indulge them in sentimental and meaningless pillow talk.

After realising that he is extremely unpopular, François Molière has decided not to contest the upcoming presidential elections. He has chosen instead to live a life of hedonistic, drunken debauchery, while delegating most of his authority to the French prime minister.

Salvatore Berlosconti, Italy's richest man, has been friends with François Molière for more than thirty years. They were introduced at the former's Naples bordello. In common with all Italian politicians of his and earlier generations, Berlosconti rose through the political ranks in that most orthodox Italian manner: bribery, corruption, blackmail, and violence. He retains his Capri establishment out of a sense of nostalgia and sentimentality. On entering politics he had decided to sell the rest of his network of knocking shops to that ancient ancestor of the private equity firm, the Mafia.

Now in his mid eighties, Berlosconti remains sprightly and is even considering making a comeback on to the political stage. Surprisingly, for a man of his age, his libido has barely diminished, although his amorous antics have had to be tempered due to bouts of barely controllable incontinence and flatulence. François Molière is perhaps unaware of just how brave he is in sharing the same enclosed space.

Berlosconti shares much in common with the previous pimp who governed Italy: the Emperor Caligula, a lunatic with delusions of divinity, who married his horse and impregnated his younger sister.

Although his sanity has always been in question, no evidence exists of Berlosconti ever marrying a horse. Certainly, he has delusions of godhood and believes himself to be divinely irresistible to women. While he was cleared by a court, sixty years previously, of inappropriate conduct with his fifteen-year-old sister, suspicion still abounds, particularly as he had not only cited but demonstrated that often-used Italian axiom employed by most convicted deviants in Italy that 'an Italian virgin was a girl who could outrun her brother'.

Outside of Hollywood, one would be hard-pressed to find two Lotharios more deserving of the label who often shared a bathtub at the same time.

François Molière's mobile phone rings. He answers it.

"Err ... *Bonjour François, c'est* Berkeley," says Berkeley Hunt, in an appalling French accent.

157

"Ah, Berkeley. *Bonjour, mon ami. Comment ça va?*" replies the Frenchman, in an alcoholic semi-stupor.

"Right, enough of the Frog-speak. You know mine's not very good. Look I need to ask you a favour."

"*Bien sur, mon ami.* Anything for you," it is the French president's standard reply to anyone who asks him for anything while he is inebriated.

"Well, it's like this. You know we may be having a bit of a contretemps with the Argies shortly, and if things don't go according to plan, we may need to borrow one of your aircraft carriers. So how about it? Just say yes, and our military chaps can work out the details." Berkeley Hunt is not keen to have an extended conversation with the French president.

"Of course, *mon ami.* Just tell your admiral to contact our chief of staff tomorrow."

"Excellent. Right, well, I think I'll be off—"

The French president interrupts him. "No, no, no … wait one moment," Berkeley Hunt waits impatiently for François Molière to return to the phone.

"*Ciao*, Berkeley," cries out Salvatore Berlosconti down the phone.

Berkeley Hunt's heart sinks. He loathes the former Italian president. Indeed, the feeling is mutual.

"*Ciao*, Salvatore," he replies without much enthusiasm. Both men only have a smattering of the other's language, and so are able to insult each other with relative impunity.

"How is that sister of yours? The one with the big nose – Ruth," asks Berlosconti in Italian.

Recognising his sister's name, Berkeley Hunt replies, "Yes, Ruth is fine, thank you. She's in Istanbul."

"Istanbul? What's she doing there? Selling herself into a harem to the highest bidder? Or has your brother got her servicing his clients while he picks their pockets?" replies Berlosconti in Italian, and then laughs.

Sensing that the former president has said something rude about his sister, Berkeley Hunt replies, "Well, it was nice talking to you, Salvatore. *Ciao*, you fat flatulent pig. I hope your haemorrhoids explode soon."

"*Ciao*, Berkeley," replies Berlosconti. Both men put down their phones.

Berkeley Hunt sighs.

"God, as if it isn't bad enough having to talk to Molière, who no doubt by tomorrow will have forgotten our conversation, I have to put up with that vulgar old wop pimp."

"Rather you than me, old son," replies Nick Lafarge, drily.

There is a knock at the door and Admiral Turgidly enters, accompanied by Sir Humbert Windrush, Permanent Secretary at the Ministry of War. At fifty years of age Sir Humbert still lives with his mother. He is that new breed of senior civil servant destined to take early retirement and be recruited by one of the large accountancy or law firms for his talents in time-wasting, procrastination, and obfuscation.

For the time being the Ministry of War finds itself fortunate, and indeed is grateful, to have Sir Humbert as the Permanent Secretary. Since the beginning of his tenure, and unlike other important government departments, the Ministry of War's reputation has remained unaffected. No Parliamentary committee nor judicial investigation has ever summoned Sir Humbert to explain the incompetency, ineptitude, and financial mismanagement of his department. This could be due to his peculiar set of personal attributes: an abundance of dandruff, noxious foot and body odour, nausea-inducing halitosis, and almost incessant, fetid flatulence. Admiral Turgidly is careful to stand downwind of the air conditioning and, even at a distance of twenty feet, Nick Lafarge and Berkeley Hunt wrinkle their noses.

"Yes, Admiral, what is it?" asks the prime minister.

"A couple of things, Prime Minister … First, I've issued the orders to HMS *Argo* and will be forwarding the latest intelligence reports to them later today. Second, I was a little concerned at your suggestion earlier today that we could somehow bring our nuclear deterrent into play if things don't go according to plan."

Berkeley Hunt has no intention of using nuclear weapons. However, he has only ever met Sir Humbert on one previous occasion, and it is not often that he gets the opportunity of trying to impress someone new. He stands up, puffs out his chest, takes hold of the lapels on his jacket, and in a less than convincing attempt at Churchillian rhetoric, begins.

"Well, Admiral, in fraught times a great leader sometimes needs to wave a big stick about to show his adversary that he's not mucking about and means business."

"Prime Minister, are you seriously considering threatening the Argentinians with nuclear retaliation, or even a pre-emptive strike?" asks a worried Admiral Turgidly.

"If needs be, absolutely," replies Berkeley Hunt, with seemingly genuine conviction and seriousness.

"Have you lost your head?" shouts Nick Lafarge.

The admiral, who is becoming more concerned, replies, "Prime Minister, just threatening a non-nuclear power will get us into deep water with the UN. And there's the question of international law, then there's the Americans—"

"In time of war the law falls silent, Admiral," interrupts the prime minister with as much bombast as he can summon.

"What?" asks a confused Nick Lafarge.

"Plutarch," replies Berkeley Hunt, both confidently and pompously.

"Cicero, actually," interrupts the admiral.

"Cicero? Yes, yes, of course that's what I meant," replies Berkeley Hunt, trying to cover up his ignorance.

"Look, Admiral, will you tell him, or shall I?" enquires Sir Humbert Windrush, with more than a touch of impatience and boredom.

Sir Humbert is somewhat annoyed at having been summoned by Admiral Turgidly to Whitehall at short notice on his day off. He was rather looking forward to attending his club and indulging his favourite hobby later that day.

He is a member of what is probably the most exclusive gentleman's club in the world, a club that counts national and international dignitaries amongst its membership. Originally founded by operatives of the British secret service, the club could not otherwise exist without their collaboration. Unbeknownst to the British taxpayer, and contrary to popular belief, the covert surveillance operations of the security services in the UK exist not entirely for reasons of national security but also to cater to the tastes of Sir Humbert and his fellow club members.

Sir Humbert, like most foul-smelling men who've never had the opportunity to copulate, at least not with a human being, is an avid voyeur and peeping Tom. He is feeling particular aggrieved, as he suspects that he will miss the club's latest instalment and live screening of the goings-on in the ladies' changing room at a well-known London gymnasium.

Admiral Turgidly clears his throat and replies to Sir Humbert.

"Err ... I'll tell him. Well, you see, it's like this, Prime Minister. We don't err ... *actually* ... have a nuclear deterrent."

"What? Don't be ridiculous. We've got four nuclear submarines bristling with nuclear missiles. I've been on board one of them," replies Berkeley Hunt sceptically.

"We do have one missile submarine, but it doesn't have any real missiles. We just get it to sail about for a bit, and make sure the media are there to take pictures. That's tended to keep people off the scent," replies the admiral.

161

"No, no, no. I've seen two submarines on the news channels berthed side by side," replies Berkeley Hunt.

"The other one is just a shell, with changing nameplates. It gets winched up and down from time to time, to make it look as though we've got a fleet," replies the admiral.

Sir Humbert interjects. "The fact is, Prime Minister, we can't afford a nuclear deterrent. Over the last fifty years we've written off billions in failed and cancelled projects. Even the successful ones, like our attack submarines and the Javelin sea-skimming missile system, have gone billions over budget. Naturally, we've filled this black hole in our accounts by transferring the budget from our nuclear deterrent programme. We'd worked out a plan about ten years ago to get the funding to build a real fleet of nuclear armed submarines ... but the government had to bail out the banks during the financial crisis, so there simply wasn't the money."

"Is this some sort of joke?" interrupts Nick Lafarge, with a mixture of bemusement and incredulity.

"I'm afraid not, Deputy Prime Minister. And there's more," begins Sir Humbert. "The number of civil servants in the Ministry of War far exceeds the number of military personnel in our armed forces. Now to reduce this number is going to cost billions in redundancies, pensions for early retirement, and a whole raft of other expenses. Then there's our contract with Lockwood, the American defence contractor. They've sold us a rather large pup in the form of the most expensive and useless aircraft ever to be made, for service on our aircraft carriers. So, for the foreseeable future, a nuclear deterrent is out of the question."

"Hold on a minute ... How come the National Audit Office haven't twigged what's going on?" asks Nick Lafarge.

"With the help of the accountants Young & Waterman, and their expertise in creative accounting and falsifying audit documentation, we've managed to bamboozle the NAO for some time," replies Sir Humbert.

"No doubt they charge us heftily for keeping schtum," says the deputy prime minister, cynically.

"Actually, Deputy Prime Minister, they charge us no fee at all. But they have an arrangement with the tax office to allow a couple of their more aggressive tax avoidance schemes to pass unhindered," replies Sir Humbert.

"Why wasn't I told before about our nuclear deterrent, or lack of?" asks Berkeley Hunt, confused and not a little annoyed.

"It's always been handled on a need-to-know basis, sir," replies the admiral.

Now shouting, Berkeley Hunt replies, "I'm the bloody prime minister. Don't you think I need to know?"

"Frankly, no, Prime Minister," replies the admiral. "It would skew your judgement in international relations. And, of course, we wouldn't want to encourage some gung-ho prime minister to engage in reckless bluffing by threatening someone with nuclear annihilation. It would be extremely dangerous, and could even expose the truth—"

Nick Lafarge, who is a little vexed himself, interjects and says forcefully, "I would have thought, Admiral, that threatening someone with nuclear annihilation and *not* knowing that we couldn't in fact annihilate them ... would be far more dangerous!"

"Only if a prime minister were threatening a first strike against a nuclear power, so it is a calculated risk. Fortunately, until now we haven't had one who's been idiot enough to do so," replies the admiral.

"What's that supposed to mean?" replies Berkeley Hunt, feeling decidedly slighted.

On sensing that he has made something of a faux pas, Admiral Turgidly backtracks.

"Err ... what I mean is that the issue concerning the use of nuclear weapons has arisen only once before."

Sir Humbert cuts in. "Yes, I believe that during the last Falkens conflict, when things weren't going so well, Mrs Thatcher wanted to do the same thing: bomb Buenos Aires. I hate to think what she would have done had she found out the truth."

"So why are you telling me now? Argentina isn't a nuclear power," enquires Berkeley Hunt.

"Indeed, Prime Minister. But, with international tensions as high as they are, we thought it best to let you know. If you were to threaten Argentina that might just bring the Russians into play, and that … *would* be dangerous. I'm sure you wouldn't want to start World War Three without knowing the truth," replies Admiral Turgidly.

"So who else knows about this charade?" asks Berkeley Hunt.

"Obviously all my predecessors for the last forty years, many of whom are dead," replies Sir Humbert.

"My predecessors too, Prime Minister, many of whom are also dead. Of course a number of our counterparts in the US military and the War Department … and every president since Ronald Reagan has been aware of the situation," replies the admiral.

"Are you telling me that US presidents for forty years have known about our nuclear deterrent and that British prime ministers haven't?"

"Well, Prime Minister, that just goes to show that it's been a very closely guarded secret. If *you* and former prime ministers didn't know you can bet that the Russians and the Chinese don't know either," replies Admiral Turgidly confidently.

****

It is approaching early evening in Moscow. Vladimira Pushkin is on the phone to Poota Bastardo. She is becoming bored with the Argentine president's incessant whining.

164

"I am extremely concerned, Mrs Pushkin, at the possibility of British nuclear retaliation when we recapture the Malvinas, or even the possibility of a pre-emptive first strike."

"Do you really believe that the British would attack a non-nuclear power with nuclear weapons? For goodness' sake, woman, the repercussions for them would be disastrous ... far more so than the loss of the Malvinas," replies the Russian president angrily.

Equally angrily, Poota Bastardo replies, "Well, that's easy for you to say. You're not taking the risk of being vaporised in your office by a British nuclear missile. How can you say what that idiot Berkeley Hunt may or may not do? The man is totally unpredictable. I may be compelled to do your bidding for the present, but being blown up is not a risk I want to take."

Vladimira Pushkin sighs inwardly. She did not want to have to reveal one of her most important intelligence discoveries, but her deadline is looming and she is becoming bored and irritated with her Argentinian counterpart.

"Dear Poota," she begins, "I can guarantee that there will be no British nuclear strike against Argentina—"

"How can you possibly guarantee such a thing?" snaps the Argentinian president.

Barely keeping control of her temper at the interruption, the Russian president replies, "Dear Poota, I can guarantee that there will be no British nuclear strike against Argentina, because the British *do not* possess a nuclear deterrent. My best agent was able to *literally* sweat that information out of an impeccable, indeed unimpeachable, source." And then, laughing, she says, "Although he was once, in fact, impeached."

"It seems rather unlike you, Mrs Pushkin, to accept the word of a single intelligence agent on a matter of such significance and gravity," replies Poota Bastardo.

"The agent, my dear Poota, was *me*. I uncovered this intelligence nearly twenty years ago when I worked at the Foreign Intelligence Bureau."

Vladimira Pushkin smiles to herself and gazes in to the distance through the windows as she recalls a few pleasant days spent in Aspen, Colorado, nearly twenty years previously.

She is in a log cabin lying on a hearthrug in front of a wood fire. In spite of the heat her nakedness is covered by a full-length mink coat. Lying next to her, and also naked, is a man who, although nearly twenty years her senior, is legendary in Washington DC for his sexual prowess and stamina. Pushkin sighs contentedly, pushes her fingers and palm through the man's hairy chest, and then says,

"*Dorogoy* (darling) … One more time."

The man replies, "Hold on, honey. Need to get some more juice in the tank." He rolls up another cannabis joint, lights it, and inhales deeply.

"Is there anyone special in your life, Jimmy?" asks Pushkin.

"What? Apart from me, you mean?" replies Jimmy.

Pushkin laughs and then goes on.

"What would your wife say if she knew about me?"

"Hilary? Hell, honey, she'd give you a medal. She hasn't let me anywhere near her since nine months before Everton was born, and that was fifteen years ago."

"What was it you were saying about the British, *dorogoy*?" asks Pushkin innocently.

"The Brits? Yeah, well, they always do what we tell 'em." He inhales deeply once more from the joint. "Cos they're too broke to afford their own nukes," continues Jimmy Poinswatter.

Vladimira Pushkin's reverie is interrupted by the shrill whining tone of Poota Bastardo.

"How can you be certain that your source was not a plant?"

166

Replying angrily, Pushkin says, "What would be the point of planting such information? Poota, clearly you have no concept of nuclear diplomacy and strategy. Enough of this nonsense. I expect you to carry out your instructions on schedule. Do I make myself clear?"

The threat in the Russian president's voice is unmistakable.

****

It is evening in the South Atlantic. HMS *Argo* is patrolling in its designated zone. Lieutenant Commander Smedley Butler of the United States Navy has gone three days without the medication that keeps his claustrophobia in check, and he is now quite nauseous as he staggers through the main corridor of the boat. As he passes the communications room the petty officer on duty calls out to him,

"Commander Butler, sir, would you mind taking this action message to the captain? It's just that I'm a bit behind in my decoding, sir."

"Sure," replies Butler as he takes hold of the message. He staggers off down the corridor while trying to read the message, which reads:

ACTION MESSAGE 114/23: From CinC Fleet to Captain HMS Argo. Be advised ...

Butler is unable to read the message any further as he is overcome by a bout of nausea. He makes his way to the nearest toilet, where he vomits violently. Unnoticed by him, the action message falls into the bowl. He flushes the toilet and makes his way back shakily to his quarters, where he collapses on to his bunk.

An hour later Butler awakes from his tortured sleep. He gets out of his bunk and splashes some water over his face. After changing his shirt and straightening the rest of his uniform he makes his way unsteadily to the mess. He helps himself to a glass of water and takes

167

a seat at the nearest vacant table. His nausea has subsided, but after a few minutes he begins to fall into something akin to a catatonic state.

A young officer joins him at the table. The officer is clearly thrilled, never having been previously in combat. He begins to chatter away excitedly, and so fails to notice Butler's mental state.

"Well, Commander Butler, sir, looks like we could be going into action soon. Must say I'm looking forward to it tremendously. Feel sorry for you, though. Must be terribly disappointing to be relieved of duty and not have your finger on the trigger, eh? Still, you'll get a front row seat, what?

"You know, my old man was on board the *Splendid* in the last punch-up with the Argies. Only managed to torpedo a few whales, though. Hopefully we can send a flat-top or two to the deep six and the rest of 'em packing.

"Well, got to go, on duty in five minutes. Toodle-oo."

The young officer finishes his drink and leaves. Smedley Butler remains, totally oblivious to the entire monologue.

Day Twenty-Four

It is morning in Buenos Aires. Admiral Fellatcio walks nervously past two Russian guards in the presidential palace. He knocks on the president's door and then enters her office. After walking up to her desk he hands Poota Bastardo a file.

"Good," says the Argentine president. "So the fleet will sail tomorrow evening?"

"Yes. Look, Madam President, this is the first opportunity we have had in some time to communicate privately, and I have to say that I have grave misgivings about this operation," replies the admiral.

"What do you mean, Admiral? A swift victory will strengthen your and my position at home considerably," she counters.

"I'm not so sure. In spite of your recent financial generosity towards the people they are nonetheless restless. The army has had to deal with three riots in the last two days, and using Russian troops to help them has only incensed the population more."

"All of that will change once the Malvinas are back under our control. I'm certain of it," she replies.

"And if we lose?" asks the admiral, "What do you think will happen to the both of us then? Nothing good, that's for certain."

"For a number of years now, Admiral, you have been assuring me that our military capabilities are the best in South America."

"Certainly that is true, but the British military is amongst the best in the world."

"So what?" she retorts angrily. "The British haven't even reinforced the Malvinas, and soon it will be too late to do so."

"And I'm still hopeful that they will," replies the admiral impassively.

"What? Are you serious?" responds a stunned Poota Bastardo.

"I have been in contact for some time with British Intelligence and the British Chief of Defence Staff ..."

"Do you realise what you are saying? I could have you arrested and court-martialled. If Pushkin found out she'd have you eliminated. You are—"

The Argentine president is interrupted forcefully by the admiral. "The British will already have in place two, possibly three submarines by now to intercept and destroy our fleet—"

It is now Poota Bastardo's turn to interrupt. "That will not happen. The Russians have assured us that their anti-submarine technology can locate and destroy any submarine long before it is any threat to our ships."

Admiral Fellatcio removes his cap and mops his brow with a handkerchief. After replacing his cap he asks with quiet composure, "And you believe them? Because I don't."

Poota Bastardo is quiet and reflective for a few moments. The admiral continues to press the point.

"The Russians have never elaborated on nor provided us with any meaningful technical data on the British *Argo*-class submarine. In my view they know as little as we do about its capabilities."

"What are you saying, Admiral?" She is now beginning to have doubts herself.

"If the British reinforced the Malvinas we both know that the fleet and amphibious assault commanders would not launch an attack against the islands. Pushkin could do little to us in those circumstances. On the other hand, if our fleet were destroyed by British submarines, our own people, who are already disaffected, would revolt against us. And this may very well suit Pushkin's agenda, whatever that may be."

"You could be right, but I don't see what we can do about it. Believe me when I tell you that I can't just tell her I'm not going invade the islands," she replies anxiously.

"Look, I've been working on a plan for nearly two weeks. I think it'll work and get us out of this mess, but we need—"

The admiral is interrupted by gunfire in the streets. Poota Bastardo becomes alarmed.

"What's that?" she cries.

"Probably another demonstration, or a riot. I'll go and find out," replies the admiral, as he leaves the room.

****

It is early evening at Number 10 Downing Street. Berkeley Hunt is in his office. He is pacing up and down and feeling decidedly apprehensive at the prospect of an inevitable military engagement, for which he knows he will bear the brunt of responsibility. There is a knock at his door. Sir Percy Talleewacker enters.

"I think you had better turn on the news," he says.

Berkeley Hunt reaches for his remote control and presses the button for the news channel. A newscaster is announcing that civil disturbances and rioting are taking place all over Argentina, and that Poota Bastardo and several top military personnel may have been killed. It appears that a full-scale revolution is underway.

"Well, it looks like our little Falkens problem could be over," says Sir Percy.

Berkeley Hunt breathes a sigh of relief.

"Thank God for that," he says.

"It's probably an idea to have another COMA meeting in any event, Prime Minister."

"Quite. Well, you organise it, Sir Percy." Sir Percy nods and leaves the room.

Berkeley Hunt goes back to his desk and sits down. After exhaling deeply once more he slumps back into his chair, the signs of strain ebbing away from his face. He remains motionless and silent for a few moments, allowing the sense of relief to course through his body and dispel all the tension that he has been feeling for the last few days. He hasn't felt this relaxed since the last really good thrashing that Penny administered to him six weeks ago.

He smiles, rubs his hands together, and says to himself, "Right. Time for a good celebratory spanking, methinks."

Just as he is about to pick up his phone and call Penny it rings.

"Are you watching the news, Humpty?" asks Mike Hunt.

"Err ... yes, a few minutes ago."

"Well, what's going on?"

"Not entirely sure. Obviously some sort of rebellion. Anyway, got a meeting shortly to find out."

"And what are you going to do about it?" There is a distinct tinge of menace in Mike Hunt's voice.

Berkeley Hunt becomes slightly unnerved and replies, "What do you expect me to do about it?"

"You were supposed to start a war," replies his brother, with even more menace in his voice.

"What? No I wasn't. You asked – no, blackmailed – me into not reinforcing the Falkens, which is exactly what I did," replies Berkeley Hunt, now quite perplexed.

"Not so, Humpty. The consequences of so doing were to bring about a war, which now looks unlikely. So you've failed, so far, in your task."

"Look, Bruiser, you can't pin this on me. I'm not responsible for the Argies having a punch-up amongst themselves in their own country."

"Fair enough," replies Mike Hunt in what appears to be a reasonable tone.

"What?" replies his surprised brother.

"Fair enough. You're right. You're not responsible. So if you'll just write me a cheque for fifty million dollars we'll call it quits."

"What? You know I don't have fifty million dollars, and what do I owe you fifty million for anyway?"

"Fifty million is what I'm down in trading on the markets, due to your incompetence in not being able to start even the smallest, most insignificant of wars."

"Look, what do you expect me to do? Start attacking sovereign countries for no reason whatsoever?"

"Why not? You're the prime minister. If Teflon Tony did it so can you. Nuke someone if you have to."

"Err ... actually, I can't do that either. Anyway, if I did order an unprovoked attack on a sovereign state I'd end up in chokey just as surely as I would for money laundering."

"If Teflon Tony and George Rush didn't get nicked then neither will you. But, if you did, you'd end up in that prison next to The Hague, where all the war criminals and former heads of government get sent. The one with the à la carte menu, swimming pool, tennis courts, Jacuzzi, and conjugal visits. You'd do about five years. On the other hand, if you get done for money laundering, you'd do at least twenty years in a rat hole in Arkansas or Alabama. With your ring-piece getting pounded daily, your haemorrhoids will press charges against you for grievous bodily harm.

"I don't care who you start a war with. Bomb the bloody French for all I care! No one will mind that, but you'd better think of something pretty quick."

Mike Hunt slams down the phone. Berkeley Hunt slouches forward and holds his head in his hands.

****

It is late evening in Bayswater, London. Berkeley Hunt is sitting on a sofa in Penny's living room. He is, unsurprisingly, quite morose. Sitting a few feet away to the side in his motorised wheelchair is the world-renowned Nobel Prize-winning cosmologist, Professor Hawksworth. Berkeley Hunt is unable to resist stealing a furtive glance at the professor. In spite of the fact that he has other things on his mind, Berkeley Hunt can't help wondering what sort of service it is that Penny provides for this pillar of academia.

There is the sound of a whip cracking in Penny's bedroom, accompanied by agonised yelps and moans, followed by Penny's voice barking out abuse and expletives.

"Rough day?" enquires Professor Hawksworth. Professor Hawksworth cannot speak. His words are conveyed via his laptop, which is attached to his wheelchair. These are then relayed through an electronic voice synthesiser.

"Just a bit," huffs Berkeley Hunt.

"Well, there's nothing like quality rest and relaxation. And no one dishes it out quite as well as dear Penny, a true angel of mercy," replies Professor Hawksworth, just as the crack of a whip and a loud yell is heard from the bedroom.

"Tell me," asks the professor, "do you see anything of that school friend of yours? The other chap who was also prime minister."

"Who, Dave? Haven't seen him for a bit, actually. As you know, he had a bit of a breakdown after the Brexit vote. Hasn't been the same since. In fact, if anything he's getting worse. He insists on people calling him 'Marjorie'. I hear he's thinking about having a gender reassignment operation."

"So I take it that means you and he will no longer be bum chums?" enquires the professor.

"What? Why do people think we were ever bu — that?"

"I suppose it's because you and he were always seen loitering around all the public toilets on the campus together."

"For the love of God. I give up," cries Berkeley Hunt, shaking his head.

"You know, we're running a book on you two at the faculty to see which one of you gets voted as the worst prime minister in history," says the professor.

"Really?" replies Berkeley Hunt drily, and quite unamused.

"But don't worry," replies Professor Hawksworth. "I recently met a village idiot in Wales who thinks you're quite a good one. Ha, ha, ha."

"That was funny, Professor. And they call you a genius ... That's a far bigger joke!"

"What was it you got? A pass degree in philosophy and politics? Ha, ha, ha," counters Professor Hawksworth.

"Well, Professor, if you're such a bloody genius, perhaps you can tell me how to start a war and end it without getting anyone killed, eh? Try that for size, Einstein!" retorts Berkeley Hunt with a mixture of anger and frustration.

"Einstein? He was a cretin! You really are a dunderhead. It's very simple, dear boy. You declare war on a country and then do nothing to them. After a while you surrender."

"That's not particularly helpful, Professor," replies Berkeley Hunt, who was half hoping that Professor Hawksworth may say something vaguely useful to help solve his problem.

"Well, be more specific, then."

"I need our adversary to declare war on us too."

"Why didn't you say so, you idiot? Hmm, that's a bit trickier."

Professor Hawksworth is silent for a few moments, as he mulls the problem over.

"Right, I've got it," begins Professor Hawksworth. "You do something similar to what the Argies did in the last Falkens conflict."

"Well, what's that?"

"Are you always in such a hurry?"

"Only when I'm desperate," mutters Berkeley Hunt under his breath.

"Anyway," continues Professor Hawksworth, "you invade some piece of fairly worthless territory, preferably an island, which is barely populated. It should have some functional but currently unused infrastructure. Once the population know that they've been invaded they'll inform their government.

"You destroy the infrastructure and take some of the population prisoner. You inform their government that the whole thing was some terrible mistake once they declare war on you, and that you accidentally attacked the wrong island as part of some sort of military exercise. Something like that.

"Send them a large cheque, and that should be the end of it. In theory it works, but it's not foolproof ... which is unfortunate, as I doubt there's a bigger fool than you. Ha, ha, ha."

The door to Penny's bedroom opens. Dressed in her dominatrix outfit she strides out and shouts, "Right, which one of you miserable cockroaches is next?"

Day Twenty-Five

It is 8 a.m. at Number 10 Downing Street. Berkeley Hunt yawns and rubs his eyes. Having forgone his weekly thrashing by Penny, he has spent most of the night and morning working away at the Ministry of War, and then at the headquarters of CinC Fleet. Berkeley Hunt has formulated a plan, the consequences of which he hopes will both keep him out of prison and satisfy his brother.

His mobile phone rings, and Berkeley Hunt shudders as he sees his brother's name illuminated on the screen.

"Well, what are you doing to sort out my little problem?" asks Mike Hunt. The cold impassiveness of his voice unsettles Berkeley Hunt even more. Mike Hunt continues, his voice rising to a crescendo, "I'm a hundred million dollars down. In a couple of days, at this rate, I'll be in margin call. Do you know what that means? I'll have to start selling things. I might have to move to Putney – or worse, Islington, with all the Commies and Trots!"

"Err … Look, Bruiser, I've been working on a plan, and by tomorrow I think I can pull it off. I'm pretty certain I can get a war going, but I don't think we can keep it going for all that long."

"How long?"

"Well … um, three … maybe four days."

"What? That's not good enough."

"Look, Bruiser, if it's not good enough then it's not good enough! Having me carted off to chokcy, though, isn't going to get you your money back, is it?" shouts Berkeley Hunt in an unusually forthright manner.

There is a long silence at the other end of the phone.

"Just make sure your plan works, Humpty," replies Mike Hunt and hangs up.

There is a knock at the door and Admiral Turgidly enters.

"Ah, Admiral," begins Berkeley Hunt, "thank you for coming. I've called you here for a private meeting, but first have you stood down HMS *Argo*?"

"I was about to, Prime Minister, with your permission," replies the admiral.

"Not quite yet: in another forty-eight hours, I think. There's something I need you to do," begins Berkeley Hunt, as he moves to his desk and opens up a map of the South Atlantic.

"I understand our Antarctic survey vessel, HMS *Odyssey*, is about here by now. Is that correct, Admiral?" he says, pointing to a spot on the map.

"Yes, that's about right, Prime Minister."

"And there's a contingent of marines from the Mountain & Arctic Warfare Detachment on board, fully armed, and with explosives?"

"Twelve, to be exact, Prime Minister," replies the admiral.

Berkeley Hunt points to another spot on the map and goes on,

"This island here … I believe that it has a mothballed whaling station, administered by the Argentine navy. There's also a lighthouse manned by a caretaker and his wife. Am I correct?"

"I believe so," replies the admiral.

"Good. six hours sailing at full steam should get the marines there, and then I want you to land them on the island, capture the lighthouse, and then blow it up, along with the whaling station. Make sure no harm comes to the caretaker, nor his wife."

Admiral Turgidly's jaw drops, and he stares at Berkeley Hunt with wide-eyed disbelief before replying, "I'm sorry, sir, but I'm confused. Attacking Argentine territory and destroying their property is, in effect, a declaration of war."

"Indeed," replies Berkeley Hunt impassively.

Admiral Turgidly is even more taken aback.

"Have you considered, Prime Minister, the reaction of the Argentinians to your actions? Being attacked by a foreign power may just get them to stop fighting amongst themselves. Even with their senior military commanders probably all dead they could, in their outrage, decide to launch an invasion of the Falkens. And they could do it immediately."

"It's certainly a possibility," replies Berkeley Hunt, in a remarkably sanguine tone.

"Even if declaring war on Argentina were legal, and there were some rhyme or reason for so doing, we would be attacking a completely worthless target we have no hope of holding with only twelve men – even though they're commandos."

"Well, we won't have to hold it for long," replies Berkeley Hunt.

Admiral Turgidly is more than a little amazed at Berkeley Hunt's calm demeanour. He is now becoming quite concerned at the possible ramifications of the prime minister's proposal. The admiral replies,

"Are you proposing to debate this with the Cabinet or in Parliament? Because I have to say that I'm certain they would not agree to such an eccentric plan."

"Of course not, and we don't have to tell Parliament because it will be treated as a special forces operation."

"A special forces operation ... to achieve what, exactly?" exclaims the admiral.

Shrugging his shoulders, Berkeley Hunt replies, "I don't know. Think of something."

"What? What do you mean, 'Think of something'? No, no, I won't do it."

"Why not?"

"Because it's insane. And you haven't given me any sort of vaguely credible reason, nor any explanation," replies Admiral Turgidly, almost shouting.

Berkeley Hunt continues with a surprising show of composure.

"Insane, eh, Admiral? Not quite. You, however, have surpassed insanity."

"What do you mean?" asks the admiral indignantly.

"Our so-called nuclear deterrent. Tell me, Admiral, how long have you known about it? Since your days as head of the Submarine Service, no doubt – a conspiracy that would make the Dolphin Square scandal look like a traffic violation! You know, I might just have to inform Parliament about the whole sorry charade."

"Yes, well, Prime Minister, the whole thing will be on your head, not to mention that you would be seriously compromising our national security. And, with respect, you would probably have to resign for appearing to be incompetent for not having known."

"As most people already think I'm incompetent I'll probably have to resign soon enough anyway. And, frankly, Admiral, it would be a blessed release. As for the whole thing being on my head … I think not.

"On the other hand you, along with a dozen other servants of the Crown are guilty of conspiracy, fraud, and the misappropriation of monies from Her Majesty's Treasury, to name but a few felonies. What do you think the penalty for that is likely to be?" replies Berkeley Hunt, fixing the admiral with an uncharacteristically steely glare.

Admiral Turgidly twists his neck up and sideways and feels his collar. An outbreak of perspiration on his forehead causes him to remove his cap and dab his brow with a handkerchief.

"I … err … see your point," he says, now sounding quite chastened. He is silent for a few moments and then continues, "I'll… ah … go and give the orders to HMS *Odyssey* right away."

180

"Good. Don't worry, Admiral. It'll be our little secret." Admiral Turgidly leaves.

Berkeley Hunt turns around and places both hands on his desk and leans on to it wearily. He blows out his cheeks and says to himself, "If the worst comes to the worst ... Well, I don't suppose the next five years in a luxury prison in Holland will be all that bad. I wonder if they'll let Penny visit?"

****

It is 9 p.m., GMT minus three hours, in the South Atlantic. The captain of HMS *Argo* is in the Con (Control Room). Although it is not yet time to relieve the executive officer from his watch the captain, like the rest of the crew, is anxious, as the boat remains on high alert.

"Sir!" Shouts the sonar operator, "I have multiple contacts ... seven – no, eight contacts, bearing, two, four, zero. Range: one hundred miles. Course: zero, three, five, making two zero knots."

The captain and the executive officer move over to the sonar operator's console and examine his screen.

"It must be them, sir, sailing in close formation at that speed. It can only be a naval task force," remarks the executive officer.

"I agree, Number One, but what are they doing there? Why are there only eight of 'em, and why are they heading nor-nor-east? And why hasn't the acoustic data processor (ADP) identified the contacts, Sonar?" says the captain.

"I don't know, sir. It *is* functioning," replies the sonar operator.

"Well, run a diagnostic," says the captain.

"Aye, sir."

"It could be, sir," begins the executive officer, "that it's the screening force, and that the amphibious assault ships are some way off to the west."

"Possibly, Number One, possibly, which leaves us with a dilemma. Do we pursue the contacts, or do we hold our position here and hope to make contact with the assault ships?"

"Pursuit, I think, sir. If we send them to the bottom the assault ships might turn tail and scarper," replies the executive officer.

"Hmm," muses the captain. "Helm," he orders, "come about to heading two, nine, zero. Make depth one hundred feet. Navigator, plot course and speed to close contacts to twenty-five miles."

****

It is midnight, GMT plus one hour, at Number 10 Downing Street. Not having slept for nearly a day, Berkeley Hunt is slumped in his chair. He is snoring away in something of a fitful sleep. His mobile rings, and he jumps out of his seat and searches for his phone in the darkness. After finally locating it he turns on his desk lamp and takes the call.

"Err … yes?"

"Well, the marines landed on the island at three o'clock this afternoon GMT. They blew up everything that was nailed down," begins Admiral Turgidly.

"The caretaker contacted the mainland before he and his wife were captured. So, if they are of a mind, the Argentinians may well plan some sort of retaliatory action, and it's possible they could have launched their invasion fleet."

"Three o'clock? Why wasn't I informed earlier?"

"We've had some communications problems with HMS *Odyssey*, Prime Minister."

"Oh, well, never mind. Withdraw the marines. And, as they've blown up his home, I suggest they take the caretaker and his wife along too," replies Berkeley Hunt.

The Day I Stopped Worrying and Learned to Love Berkeley Hunt

It is 9 a.m. in the South Atlantic, GMT minus three hours. HMS *Argo* has closed in on the eight unidentified contacts and is sailing adjacent to them on a parallel course. The captain has decided to wait and see if the suspected amphibious assault ships make an appearance before he takes action. He turns to the sonar operator and asks,

"Have you completed the second diagnostic on the ADP?"

"Yes, sir, but I can't find any fault," replies the sonar operator. The captain sighs irritably.

"Well, run another one," he says.

Lieutenant Commander Smedley Butler is in his quarters, sitting silently on his bunk. He is drifting in and out of a catatonic state. To make matters worse he is suffering hallucinations, mostly in connection with previous combat drills. He stands up, leaves his quarters, and makes his way to the mess.

In the weapons room the acting weapons officer (AWO) and weapons petty officer (WPO) are seated at their consoles. With Smedley Butler unavailable for duty, the AWO has had to undertake an extra watch since the alert was ordered. He is feeling somewhat exhausted and jaded. The WPO's stomach rumbles audibly.

"Sorry, sir," he says. "Don't know what Chef put in the vindaloo last night. Whatever it is it's been making my guts dance the cancan."

"Don't worry about it. Mine are none to good either. When we've finished you can help me fire that useless sod out of a torpedo tube. I hope we go into action soon or are stood down. I'm dying for a Turkish," replies the AWO.

In the Con the sonar operator shouts out, "Sir! I have new contacts. Six contacts. Bearing: two, nine, zero. Range: forty-five miles. Course: zero, three, five. Making two zero knots."

"Those must be the amphibious assault ships, sailing on the same course and at the same speed and twenty miles to the north-west. Can't see that they can be anything else, sir," remarks the executive officer.

"Identification?" the captain asks the sonar operator.

"Err … none, sir. Still can't get anything from the ADP," replies the sonar operator. The captain blows out his cheeks, scratches his chin, furrows his brow, and then asks, "Why are they heading nor-nor-east, Number One? It doesn't make any sense."

"My guess, sir, is that both groups are sailing in quite a wide arc in the hopes of avoiding one of our boats. They must suspect that at least one of us is here. They could possibly make thirty-five knots at a push. If they were to outrun us and enter shallow water … Well, we may not be able to stop them," replies the executive officer.

"Hmm," says the captain, mulling over the thoughts of his first officer. "You could be right, Number One." He reaches for the communications handset.

"All right, action stations!" he announces over the internal communications. There is a flurry of activity throughout the boat.

"Wepps, prepare for MRC 414 activation sequence. Helm, make depth fifty feet," he orders.

"Are we engaging the enemy, sir?" asks the executive officer."

"Not yet. If they increase speed and come about east, then yes," replies the captain.

There is a palpable sense of tension throughout the boat as the crew wait attentively at their stations. A few minutes pass, then the sonar operator shouts out, "Sir! Two contacts are disengaging from the main formation. They're coming about heading ..."

The twenty seconds that pass seem like an eternity. "... one, one, zero. They're on an intercept course — coming straight for us, sir!"

"I can't believe we've been detected," says the executive officer incredulously.

"Well, it looks that way, Number One, and it looks like we have no choice," remarks the captain drily. "Helm, come about to heading zero, nine, zero. Wepps, ready final launch sequence check," he announces into the communications handset.

"Aye, sir," comes back the reply from the AWO in the weapons room.

"Activate warhead fusing master safety for circuits one through six," instructs the captain.

"Warhead fusing master safety for circuits one through six ... Activated," replies the AWO.

"Set target acquisition mode for circuits one through three to ARML," instructs the captain.

"Target acquisition mode for circuits one through three set to ARML," replies the AWO.

"Set target acquisition mode for circuits four through six to ASML," instructs the captain.

"Target acquisition mode for circuits four through six set to ASML," replies the AWO.

"Set proximity fuse detonation for circuits one through six to impact," instructs the captain.

"Proximity fuse detonation for circuits one through six set to impact," replies the AWO.

"Set primary master switch override," instructs the captain.

"Check. Positive function all circuits," replies the AWO.

"Missile room, pressurise tubes one through six," instructs the captain.

Two minutes later the reply comes back from the missile room.

"Tubes one through six fully pressurised."

"Initiate arming key sequence," instructs the captain.

In the weapons room the AWO and WPO flick a few switches and the AWO inserts and turns the arming key. He then reaches for the firing trigger.

"Arming key activated," he reports.

"On my mark, Wepps," orders the captain, "fire tubes one through six. Four ... three ... two ..."

"Sir! priority action message on VLF radio from CinC Fleet," shouts out the communications chief petty officer (CPO) over the internal communications.

"Hold fire, Wepps," orders the captain.

Half a minute later the CPO rushes into the Con and hands the captain the message. The message reads:

PRIORITY ACTION MESSAGE 3/26:

From CinC Fleet to Captain HMS Argo.

Confirmation not received: Our action message no. 114/23.

Repeat: message 114/23.

Be advised North Korean warships.

US carrier battle group expected in your area at any time.

END MESSAGE.

The captain turns to the communications CPO and asks curtly, "Why wasn't I told about message 114/23?"

"Dunno, sir," replies the CPO, scratching his head.

"Well, we'll deal with that later. Probably a good idea to see who we are shooting at first. Wepps, deactivate arming key. Helm, periscope depth," says the captain.

"Is that wise, sir?" asks the executive officer. "If it's the enemy, and we're spotted, we'll be done for."

"And, if we sink an American or North Korean battle group, no one is going to give us the Victoria Cross, Number One," replies the captain drily.

In the weapons room:

"Thank God for that," says the AWO. "I'm off to the khazi."

"Me too," says the WPO.

The AWO turns the arming key to 'off', but does not remove it. Both men exit the weapons room and make their way hurriedly to the nearest toilet. On their way they encounter Smedley Butler but are too concerned with relieving their bowels to pay him much more than scant attention, and so fail to notice his state of mind.

"Hello, Commander. Can't really talk right now ... Dying for a Tom Tit," says the AWO. The AWO stops for a moment and regards Smedley Butler curiously, and says, "You know, you look a bit peaky. You really ought to go and see the doc," before continuing on his way to the toilet.

Three minutes later the AWO and WPO exit the toilets. There are half a dozen shudders throughout the boat.

"Bloody hell," exclaims the WPO. "We're under attack!"

****

It is 2 p.m. GMT plus one hour at Number 10 Downing Street. In the Cabinet Room Berkeley Hunt is chairing a Cabinet meeting. He is rather bored and not paying much attention, partly due to the tedious nature of the topic under discussion, but mostly because his mind is elsewhere.

It has been nearly a whole day since the marines invaded Argentine territory and destroyed their property. He is surprised as well as concerned by their lack of action, indeed reaction. He silently prays that his brother is not about to call. His thoughts are interrupted by Sir Percy Talleewacker, the Cabinet Secretary.

"Prime Minister, don't forget you have a meeting with the first minister of Scotland in ten minutes."

"What? Yes, yes, of course," replies Berkeley Hunt.

There is a knock at the door and Admiral Turgidly enters, looking distinctly uneasy. A sense of relief fills the prime minister, as he suspects that the admiral has arrived to deliver good bad news.

"Yes, Admiral, what is it?" he asks innocently.

"We've had a bit of an incident in the South Atlantic with our attack submarine HMS *Argo*."

"What sort of an incident?" enquires Berkeley Hunt, now feeling considerably more relaxed.

"Well … um, as you know, Prime Minister, we have an officer exchange programme with the United States Navy and one of their officers was serving on board HMS *Argo*. It appears that he had some sort of an episode …" Admiral Turgidly is not quite sure how to continue.

"Well, go on, Admiral," says the prime minister.

"Aah … it appears he went a bit … well … funny in the head," replies the admiral.

Now confused, Berkeley Hunts asks, "What does that mean?"

"I think the technical term is … err … mad. Yes … yes, that's it, he went mad …" replies the admiral, once again unsure as to how to continue.

"For goodness' sake, Admiral, spit it out," replies Berkeley Hunt impatiently.

"Ah ... HMS *Argo* was tracking a naval task force, seventy miles north-west of West Falken. Well ... it appears that Lieutenant Commander Smedley Butler, the US exchange officer, fired the Javelin sea-skimming missiles at the task force without authorisation, sinking an aircraft carrier, a guided missile destroyer, and badly damaging another ship, unfor—"

"Well, obviously," interrupts Berkeley Hunt, "Commander Butler attacked an Argentine invasion force and, in spite of his insanity and insubordination, we'll probably have to give him a medal." Berkeley Hunt emits a quiet laugh. There is a lot of murmuring amongst the Cabinet. Berkeley Hunt smiles broadly, as he senses he has the approval of his colleagues.

"I don't think so, Prime Minister," says Admiral Turgidly, in a tone chillingly quiet in its understatement.

"What? What do you mean?" asks Berkeley Hunt, his confidence beginning to fall away.

"Butler attacked a US carrier battle group that had been assigned to shadow a North Korean task force carrying out manoeuvres in the Atlantic. As you know, we've been aware of these manoeuvres, and the US response to them, for some time."

It is almost impossible to believe that Berkeley Hunt's pallid complexion could be any more so, as the blood drains away from his face.

"Oh, my God. That old bag in the White House will hang my knackers from the Statue of Liberty," he replies in a tone that can only be described as resigned panic. He holds his head in his hands and then allows it to drop on to the table with a loud thud.

"You're not wrong there, you gimp," says Nick Lafarge. "Why didn't you stand down HMS *Argo*? There was no danger of an invasion."

"There is some ... well ... sort of good news, I suppose," says Admiral Turgidly unsurely. Berkeley Hunt turns his head slightly

189

upwards from the table and regards the admiral out of one eye, and gestures him to continue.

"Just before he went down with his flagship, the carrier USS *Donald J Trump*, the battle group commander, Rear Admiral Ripper, thinking he had been attacked by a North Korean submarine, ordered his cruisers, without authorisation from the president, to launch a counter-attack against their fleet with tactical nuclear weapons. All but one of the North Korean ships were destroyed."

Berkeley Hunt now jumps up from his chair and shouts, "How the hell is that good news?"

"Well ... err ... it means the Americans don't realise it was us that sank their ships. And of course it does rather vindicate the effectiveness of our attack submarines and the Javelin missile system. Oh, yes, and HMS *Argo* was able to escape," replies the admiral.

"Have you gone mad as well, Admiral?" asks Berkeley Hunt, fixing Admiral Turgidly with an incredulous glare.

The admiral is spared from proffering a reply by his phone ringing.

"Yes ... yes ... right, OK ... I see," replies Admiral Turgidly in to his phone just before hanging up. He continues to address the Cabinet.

"NORAD (North American Air Defence Command) has just gone to DEFCON 3 (Defence Readiness Condition). I suggest that the Cabinet and staff evacuate immediately to the Cabinet bunker."

"Why? As you pointed out, the Americans have no reason to suspect our involvement in this," asks Berkeley Hunt. "And even if they did they're not going to nuke us ... at least I think they're not," he continues with some uncertainty in his voice.

"The Americans," begins the admiral, "have detected an increased threat level from the North Koreans. Should the North Koreans attack the United States, NATA is obliged to respond to that aggression. In that event the Chinese, under their treaty with North Korea, will launch a counter-attack against the US and NATA.

"The Americans will retaliate against the Chinese, and for good measure will probably launch a pre-emptive strike against Russia to ensure they have no spoils to collect when it's all over. In that event Russia will undoubtedly retaliate against NATA," replies Admiral Turgidly matter-of-factly.

"Bloody marvellous," cries Nick Lafarge. "It just gets better and better doesn't it, Admiral? From a possible piddling little conflict in the South Atlantic we end up with this. Cry 'Havoc'! And let slip the dogs of war."

Patricia Turbot is waiting in the main hallway of Number 10. She is a little annoyed at being kept waiting for more than hour by Berkeley Hunt, and paces up and down. She is unaware that the Cabinet have been waiting in their meeting room for their motorcade to arrive. There is a flurry of activity on the first-floor landing and stairway as the Cabinet members make their way down the stairs.

Berkeley Hunt and the rest of his colleagues walk hurriedly towards the main door. Patricia Turbot approaches the prime minister. His mind is elsewhere and he barely notices her.

"Prime Minister," she calls out, "I hope you haven't forgotten our meeting."

As he turns to her, slightly surprised, Berkeley Hunt replies, "What? Yes, err … no. Look … we'll have to have that another time."

"What's going on?" queries the Scottish first minister, a little alarmed at the sight of the entire Cabinet hurriedly exiting the building.

Berkeley Hunt grabs her by the arm and says, "You'd better come with us. I'll explain on the way."

An hour later the Cabinet motorcade arrives at the site of the Cabinet bunker. The bunker is located in Buckinghamshire and is concealed beneath several dozen metres of reinforced steel and concrete. The Cabinet members and staff alight from their motorcade and make their way to the main entrance.

The entrance is being guarded by two military policemen and their rather officious warrant officer. Berkeley Hunt, Nick Lafarge, Admiral Turgidly, and Patricia Turbot are at the head of the group, closely followed by Berkeley Hunt's personal protection officers.

"Good afternoon, gentlemen," says the warrant officer, genially. "May I ask who the lady is?"

"For goodness' sake, can't you see it's Mrs Turbot, the first minister of Scotland?" replies Berkeley Hunt irritably.

"Yes, I thought so, which …"

"Why the bloody hell did you ask, then?" shouts the prime minister.

"I'm just doing my job, Mr Hunt. We all have our place in the grand scheme of things. I may be just a lowly warrant officer and you may be the head of government, sir, but we all have our duty to do, great or small—"

"For pity's sake, just let us in, will you?" interrupts Berkeley Hunt, even more exasperated.

"By all means, sir, but Mrs Turbot will have to remain," replies the warrant officer.

"What?" queries Berkeley Hunt incredulously.

"Mrs Turbot is not a member of the Cabinet of Her Majesty's Government and is therefore not permitted access to the Cabinet bunker," replies the warrant officer.

"You're not wrong there, matey," interjects Nick Lafarge. "In fact, she's not even part of the government. Bloody hell, she doesn't even *want* to be part of the country. Right, Pat. Time for you to bugger off."

"Berkeley," cries out Patricia Turbot, fear clearly showing in her face.

"Shut up, Nick! Sergeant, for heaven's sake, man, be reasonable," implores Berkeley Hunt.

"It's not a question of reason, sir. It's a question of rules. My brother-in-law is a lawyer, and he's often telling me that reason and rules don't always go together. Besides, the bunker has only enough provisions for the Cabinet, their families, and certain designated personnel," replies the warrant officer.

"Ah, well, I've got you on that one, Sergeant, because my wife's in Switzerland, so there'll be plenty in the way of provisions," retorts the prime minister.

"That may be so, sir, but if I broke the rules for Mrs Turbot I'd have to start letting every Tom, Dick, and Harry in, wouldn't I? And then where would we be?"

"Now look here. *I'm* the prime minister, and I'm *ordering* you to let Mrs Turbot in," shouts Berkeley Hunt.

"I'm sorry, sir," comes back the firm reply from the warrant officer.

"Oh, this is absurd," says Berkeley Hunt. After grabbing hold of Patricia Turbot's hand he tries to push his way past the two MPs guarding the entrance.

"You may be the prime minister, Mr Hunt, but I must ask you to stop jostling my privates," says the warrant officer in a surprisingly cordial tone.

Berkeley Hunt turns around and calls out to one of his PPOs, "Detective, arrest that man," and points to the warrant officer.

"Err, on what charge?" replies the PPO.

"I don't know … err … obstructing a minister of the Crown," replies the prime minister. The PPO looks baffled, shrugs his shoulders, and approaches the warrant officer. All three military policemen draw their pistols, as do all three PPOs. With pistols pointed in both directions the tension is palpable to all those present.

Admiral Turgidly's phone rings.

"Yes ... OK," he says, and hangs up. He addresses those assembled as he announces, "NORAD has just gone to DEFCON 2."

"Oh, for God's sake, this is ridiculous," declares Nick Lafarge, as he moves towards Berkeley Hunt and the Scottish first minister.

"I've got an idea that'll satisfy everyone," he proclaims. As he gets into range, quick as a flash, he headbutts Patricia Turbot. She falls unconscious into a crumpled heap on the ground.

"Well ... nearly everyone." Before Berkeley Hunt can react, Nick Lafarge grabs hold of him and bundles him into the bunker. As they enter Nick Lafarge remarks, "Women ... always causing trouble."

Half an hour later Berkeley Hunt, Nick Lafarge, Admiral Turgidly, and the Cabinet Secretary, Sir Percy Talleewacker, are seated around a table in an annexe overlooking the main operations room in the Cabinet bunker.

The mood is sombre, even morose, except for Nick Lafarge, who has managed to locate a case of his favourite Scotch whisky and a carton of cigarettes, and so is happily smoking and drinking.

"Not bad here, is it?" says the deputy prime minister, a little worse for wear after consuming nearly half a bottle of whisky.

"What?" replies Berkeley Hunt irritably.

"Well, I've managed to find several cases of my favourite booze and several dozen cartons of my brand of fags. Stroke of luck, eh?" replies Nick Lafarge.

"Not really. The inventory of provisions in the bunker is specifically tailored to meet the requirements of the Cabinet," replies Admiral Turgidly.

"Really? Now if they have a whip, a pair of handcuffs, and some leather underpants, Hunt will think he's died and gone to heaven," replies Nick Lafarge, and bursts out laughing.

Berkeley Hunt gives his deputy a withering look.

An RAF officer knocks on the door and enters the room. He passes Admiral Turgidly a piece of paper.

"Prime Minister," begins Sir Percy, "don't you think we should inform the American president about the true nature of events in the South Atlantic?"

"I don't think it matters, Sir Percy," begins Admiral Turgidly. "The Americans have gone to DEFCON 1, and one of their attack submarines has just destroyed a North Korean missile submarine six hundred miles off the Pacific seaboard, but not before it managed to launch a missile. The trajectory indicates that its target is Los Angeles. I suggest that we go and take a look at the big board."

They all stand up and file out of the room. Nick Lafarge returns briefly to collect a new bottle of whisky and a couple of tumblers.

They enter the operations room, a large room filled with computer banks and individual consoles manned by various RAF personnel. The men make their way towards the big board. This consists of three extremely large computer screens attached to the front wall, on which various military dispositions are shown all over the globe.

"Multiple launch detections, Sea of Japan," announces an RAF NCO matter-of-factly.

"What's going on there?" asks Nick Lafarge.

"That'll be the Americans responding to the North Korean attack on the US mainland," replies Admiral Turgidly. They stand watching the big board for several minutes as the missiles are tracked closing in on their targets on both sides of the Pacific.

"Why haven't the Chinese reacted yet?" asks Berkeley Hunt.

"They're being pragmatic," replies Sir Percy, "They can see as well as we can that North Korea is about to be obliterated. They're probably rather pleased that a millstone is about to be removed from around their neck … and at the least they'll want to keep their powder dry, should the Americans come after them. Anyway, it's not good for business to blow up your biggest customer and your biggest debtor. On the other hand, why get involved in a nuclear war unless you absolutely have to?"

"Or why start one unless you have to, eh, Hunt?" laughs Nick Lafarge.

Berkeley Hunt turns and gives Lafarge a scornful look.

"Multiple launch detections: North-Western North Atlantic, Western Central North Atlantic, North-Western Pacific Seaboard Continental United States," announces the RAF NCO once more.

"Those aren't North Korean submarines. Those are Russians!" declares the admiral.

"What? What's that woman up to, for God's sake? She's not been attacked. This can't be part of Operation Grand Slam, surely?" queries Berkeley Hunt, almost in a panic.

"I don't believe it is, Prime Minister, but it's quite a clever strategy nonetheless …"

"Clever … What's so bloody clever about starting World War Three?" interrupts Berkeley Hunt. He is on the point of shouting.

"I think you'll find, Hunt, it was you that started World War Three," remarks Nick Lafarge.

"Just shut up, Nick," retorts Berkeley Hunt. And then he asks, "What do you mean, Admiral?"

The admiral replies, "Pushkin probably suspects that she would have been attacked sooner or later by the Americans, and by sitting on the sidelines the Chinese have presented her with something of an opportunity.

"The Americans have now been caught slightly off balance. Pushkin knows that the Americans have to keep one eye on the Chinese, so they may not be able to commit fully to a counter-attack against Russia—"

"Why not? The Americans have got more than enough firepower, surely?" interrupts Berkeley Hunt.

"Their submarines that launched against North Korea ... not only have they used up a considerable amount of their arsenal, which was overkill, one might say, but—"

"That Hilary Poinswatter ... typical woman ... always overreacting to the slightest thing," interrupts Nick Lafarge, now quite drunk.

"Will you shut up, Nick!" interjects Berkeley Hunt angrily, "Please continue, Admiral."

"As I was saying, their submarines that launched will have a depleted arsenal and will be out of reliable contact for seven hours. And, as they've given away their location, they'll be easier prey for the Russian navy and air force based in the Kamchatka Peninsula.

"Their other missile submarines at sea are probably out of position, and will not have the range to attack the Russian ICBM (intercontinental ballistic missile) complexes nor their long-range bomber bases. Their missile submarines in their bases are useless, and will be destroyed in the next ten minutes ..."

"It doesn't appear to be looking very good for our side, Admiral, does it?" interrupts Berkeley Hunt.

"I'm not sure we've got a side any more, Hunt. After all, we just blew our allies' ships out of the water not six hours ago," slurs Nick Lafarge, as he takes another large gulp of whisky.

Admiral Turgidly turns to the prime minister, and regards him with unbridled disbelief at the utter stupidity of his remark.

"No Prime Minister, it's *not very good at all.*" Continuing stoically, the admiral says, "As well as the imminent destruction of most of their submarines, their land-based command and control will also be destroyed. Unless they can launch their ICBMs and bombers before they too are shortly destroyed, they're in trouble. Even if they do, they may not have a reserve or the command structure to deal with a Russian second strike, let alone a Chinese first strike. The Russians, on the other hand, will have a very significant strategic reserve.

"In essence Pushkin has opened with a gambit: sacrificing her missile submarines to the US attack submarines in order to inflict crippling damage to US strategic nuclear capability. The US president and her staff are going to have to do some swift thinking. But I doubt she'll survive, as she's in Washington."

"Well, at least there's some good news," mutters Berkeley Hunt under his breath.

In a rare moment of lucidity Nick Lafarge remarks, albeit grudgingly because she is a woman, "I suppose we really ought to admire her – Pushkin, that is. If we had her as prime minister the world might take us seriously for a change."

"Admiral, it looks as though Pushkin has avoided attacking population and industrial centres. I don't understand. Why?" asks Sir Percy.

"There's not much point in engaging in nuclear war, Sir Percy, if you don't have any spoils to collect when it's over, particularly if you expect to take nuclear casualties yourself," replies the admiral.

"Why haven't the French done anything yet?" asks Berkeley Hunt.

"Probably 'cos they're French," hiccups Nick Lafarge.

"I suspect that like the Chinese – and us, for that matter – they're being pragmatic. After all, they haven't been attacked," replies Sir Percy. Berkeley Hunt and Admiral Turgidly exchange knowing looks.

An RAF officer approaches Admiral Turgidly and hands him a note.

"It appears," begins the admiral, "that Russian ground forces have invaded Eastern Poland. The situation seems to be confused as it appears that German troops have been occupying key Polish Garrisons, arresting and disarming Polish troops."

All four men continue to watch the big board, and in particular the Russian warheads closing in on their American targets. North Korea by now has been annihilated.

Berkeley Hunt's phone rings.

He answers it and hears, "Humpty, do you have any idea about the catastrophe that is about to happen—?"

Interrupting his brother, Berkeley Hunt replies, "Funnily enough, Bruiser ..."

"I'm serious," shouts Mike Hunt. "I'm nearly two hundred million dollars down. Do you know what that means for you? Sing Sing and sodomy!"

"Bruiser, you can sod right off. Take your money and shove it all the way—"

"You can't talk to me like that. Do you know what I'm going to do to you when I catch up with you—?"

The conversation is interrupted as an RAF NCO boldly announces, "Multiple launch detections, Norwegian Sea."

Mike Hunt continues to rant audibly but unintelligibly down the phone. Ignoring his brother and staring at the big board Berkeley Hunt exclaims, "Who the devil are they? And who the devil are they firing at?"

"I believe they're North Koreans, Prime Minister, and I think they're firing at us," replies Admiral Turgidly, who remains surprisingly calm.

"What! Why? We haven't done anything to them," replies Berkeley Hunt, now alarmed.

"We're in NATA, Prime Minister, the Americans are out of range, and we are the nearest significant target," replies the admiral.

After a couple of minutes of watching the big board Admiral Turgidly observes, "It looks as though they're *not* just going for our naval bases."

"Now we can really start laughing," slurs Nick Lafarge.

"Don't you think it's about time we retaliated, Prime Minister?" asks Sir Percy.

"With what?" sniggers Nick Lafarge.

Sir Percy responds somewhat testily, "Our nuclear deterrent, of course."

"Even if we could, there's not much left to deter ... and no one left in North Korea to deter anyway, is there?" replies the deputy prime minister.

"What does he mean?" asks Sir Percy of Berkeley Hunt, with some disquiet.

"That's the bloody irony of it, Sir Percy. If they'd known we didn't have a nuclear deterrent they'd probably have left us alone," replies Berkeley Hunt wearily.

"What? Of course we do," says the Cabinet Secretary. "We've got four submarines. I've been on board—"

"Let's not start that again. I'm sure the admiral will spell it out when this is all over," interrupts Nick Lafarge.

All four men continue to watch the big board in quiet consternation as the warheads are shown closing in on their UK targets.

"Cannon to right of them, cannon to the left of them ... I always knew there'd be some spectacular balls-up on your watch, Hunt," says Nick Lafarge, "But, I have to say, you've more than exceeded my expectations. Although you know ... I do have to thank you on the other hand ..."

"What are you talking about?" retorts the prime minister angrily.

"You see, my wife's in Los Angeles, or what's left of it. I've been trying to find a way of getting rid of her years," replies Nick Lafarge, roaring with laughter. "So have a snifter, anyway." He thrusts a tumbler into Berkeley Hunt's hand and pours out a very large measure of whisky.

A shrill scream from Mike Hunt blasts out of Berkeley Hunt's phone.

"Humpteeee! Are you there? Get back on the phone this instant, before I come over to Number 10 and kick your arse into next year."

Berkeley Hunt puts down the tumbler and goes back to his phone.

"By all means, Bruiser, cut along to Number 10. Not sure there's going to be a next year, and I'm afraid I wasn't able to start your *small, insignificant war …*"

"You useless git," screams his brother.

"But I've managed to start a rather large one instead, and I think you'll definitely get what you deserve. Although I doubt I'll get that dukedom."

"Really, are you certain?" asks Mike Hunt.

"Yes … yes, I'm pretty certain I won't get that dukedom."

"Not the dukedom, you idiot! The war."

"Oh, the war. Oh, absolutely. Cross my heart and hope to die."

"Wait … Let me go and check the markets." Mike Hunt rushes back to his computer and checks the exchanges, and then shouting into his phone says, "Yes, Humpty. Sterling has crashed, and gold has gone ballistic. You did it, you *actually* did it …"

"Yes, I did, didn't I?"

"Yes, yes, yes. I'm super, super-rich!" shouts Mike Hunt at the top of his voice. There is an almost animalistic snarl of triumph on his face. "I love you, Berkeley Hunt, you beauteeee …"

There are a series of bright flashes on the big board over London. Mike Hunt's phone line goes dead, as several thermonuclear detonations vaporise the offices of Goldstein Brothers and the rest of the capital.

All the personnel in the operations room who aren't already standing do so. All of them stare silently at the big board. Although they knew what was going to happen the shock, the horror, and the disbelief are nonetheless something of a surprise to them all.

Berkeley Hunt slowly shakes his head, then buries it in his hands for several moments. And then, struck by a sudden realisation, he looks up, open-mouthed and wide-eyed, and turns to his colleagues.

"Bloody hell," he says. "I don't believe it … He *actually* called me 'Berkeley'."

Is this the end of everything?

Printed by Amazon Italia Logistica S.r.l.
Torrazza Piemonte (TO), Italy